MW01101022

Newton

and

the Quasi-Apple

Books by Stanley Schmidt

NOVELS

*The Sins of the Fathers**

*Newton and the Quasi-Apple**

*Lifeboat Earth**

*Tweedlioop**

Argonaut

SHORT STORY COLLECTION

*Generation Gap and Other Stories**

NON-FICTION

Aliens and Alien Societies: A Writer's Guide to Creating Extraterrestrial Life-Forms

Which Way to the Future? (Selected Essays from Analog)

The Coming Convergence: The Surprising Ways Diverse Technologies Interact to Shape Our World and Change The Future

*Available from FoxAcre Press

ANTHOLOGIES EDITED

Analog Yearbook II

Analog's Golden Anniversary Anthology

Analog: Readers' Choice

Analog's Children of the Future

Analog's Lighter Side

Analog: Writers' Choice

War and Peace: Possible Futures from Analog

Aliens from Analog

Writers' Choice, Vol. II

From Mind to Mind

Analog's Expanding Universe

Unknown

Unknown Worlds

(with Martin H. Greenberg)

Analog Essays in Science

Writing Science Fiction and Fantasy

(with Gardner Dozois, Tina Lee, Ian Randal Strock, and Sheila Williams)

Islands in the Sky: Bold New Ideas for Colonizing Space (with Robert Zubrin)

Roads Not Taken: Tales of Alternate History

(with Gardner Dozois)

Newton and the Quasi-Apple

by

Stanley Schmidt

with a new afterword by the author

Newton And the Quasi-Apple

by Stanley Schmidt

Publication History:

A shorter version of this book was published under the title "Lost Newton" in the September 1970 edition of *Analog* Magazine.

Doubleday hardcover, 1975.

Popular Library paperback, 1977.

FoxAcre Press Print Editions, August 2001, April 2014.

FoxAcre Press Ebook Editions, April 2014.

copyright © 1975, 1977, 2001 by Stanley Schmidt
ISBN-13: 978-1-936771-56-1
all rights reserved

cover art and interior illustrations
N Taylor Blanchard
ntaylorblanchard.com

www.foxacre.com

Dedication

To Gordon R. Dickson,
with thanks

1

Terek woke suddenly and far too early. Only a thin sliver of faint gray light creeping through the cracks in the shutter of the small east window told him morning was even approaching. Yet something had awakened him, and he didn't know what. It was something with a prickly feeling of urgency about it. But Terek, still closer to sleep than to full wakefulness, was less conscious of that than of his annoyance at losing the thread of the dream he had been dreaming.

His mind reached back toward sleep, stretching to grasp the severed thread before it fell completely away, forever out of reach. Already it was so far gone and falling so fast that he wasn't sure what the dream had been. But it had been an exciting dream, he was sure of that much—so exhilarating and tantalizing that its promise still seemed more real and urgent than the threat which some unidentified sense had told him existed in the real world. So, momentarily relegating the real threat to second place, he chased the dream, struggling more and more frantically after its dissolving remains as he felt a growing fear that he would never be able to get it back.

Then, abruptly, *that* dissolved and he had the dream. For a few seconds he managed to hold it, turn it over in his mind, examine it from several sides. Then it vanished for good.

He hadn't had time to see it all clearly, but he had seen enough to be sure that it was the germ of something and he had not seen the last of it. He had been dreaming of the manuscripts that had been rescued from Ybhal, and in particular the yellowing pages of observations of falling bodies and the other pages of painstaking circles on circles with which some nameless old Templeman had reconstructed the paths of the Wandering Stars.

Now why, Terek thought with slight puzzlement, *should I put those two things in the same dream?* But his puzzlement at that was quickly crowded out by the excitement surrounding the one image that still remained prominent from the dream—the strange words he had found scrawled in a tiny, disguised hand in a margin of one of the pages of circle drawings: "What if Ymrek *weren't* at the center?"

He thought he saw—only dimly, so far, but he thought he saw. And he was filled with a driving eagerness to get to the monastery, where he could look again at the salvaged writings and check and pursue his ideas.

Meanwhile, the sense of something wrong persisted. What was it? Freed of what had seemed more pressing matters, his mind attuned itself in seconds to external reality. He looked around the shack's single room for anything out of order, but at first glance, at least, all seemed normal. Despite the feebleness of the light sneaking in through the shutters, the room was not really dark. Its lighting was undeniably dim, but light there was—and enough for acclimated eyes to see by—both from the phosphorescent fungi growing in patches on the walls and ceiling and floor and from the luminous icon of the dixar Kangyr in its niche in the corner. Terek's aged parents, Dajhek and Tolimra, slept as peacefully as ever these days, next to Terek on the family's straw-covered sleeping platform. Beyond them, last night's coals still glowed faintly in the fireplace, and a couple of tiny xyratl quietly and methodically cleaned up the few crumbs dropped at the evening meal.

Nowhere could Terek find anything amiss. And that fact, rather than calming the feeling of lurking danger, intensified it by making the threat seem more elusive and therefore more sinister. Quickly, Terek concentrated on other senses. Smell? Fresh straw on the sleeping platform, the damp aroma of the dirt floor and fungi, the rich many-layered scent years of cooking had made a part of the fireplace.

Nothing more. Sound? The quiet, regular breathing of his parents (though Dajhek sometimes wheezed a little), the almost inaudible scurryings of the xyratl—those were so familiar that Terek knew beyond doubt that they could not have awakened him and filled him with this haunting sensation of impending trouble.

Quietly, cautiously—both because he didn't know what he was looking for and because he didn't want to wake Dajhek and Tolimra unnecessarily—he got up off the platform and walked the two steps to the door. With care, he managed to open it far enough to look out without making noise, though of course he could do nothing about the light it let pour into the shack.

He breathed deeply of the morning air. It was cool for late summer, and mist was rising off the water where he could see it—and he could see quite a bit of it, for the shack was far out on the periphery. The shore itself was only a few yards away, and only a few other shacks, of rough-hewn wood with tall thin chimneys, blocked parts of it. The danger could be out there, but he wouldn't be able to tell until the mist burned off later in the day. As for the packed-dirt street, he could see that clearly, but it was nearly deserted. An early-rising neighbor carried two big black pots toward the neighborhood well, while a scrawny lytang—a semidomestic reptilian street scavenger—sniffed about his feet, hinting for food scraps. Two outlanders of unobvious origin strolled slowly along the rock-reinforced shore, tightly wrapped in brightly colored hooded robes and strictly minding their own business—obviously and picturesquely foreign, but neither unusual nor ominous.

Otherwise, there was nothing. Still troubled, and unsure whether to feel relieved or frustrated, Terek abandoned the search and turned to go back in.

He was pulling the door shut when he heard the cannon.

He froze in midstride at the sound. It was not particularly imposing in itself—the few guns in Yldac were old and ill-cared for, and this particular report included too much undignified sputter to be properly impressive—but there could be little doubt of what it meant. And that *was* ominous. No doubt the thing that had awakened him had been associated with that, too. Quite possibly another cannon blast, though just what it had been no longer mattered.

A low female voice came sleepily from the shadowed sleeping platform at his left. "Terek? Why are you up so early? What's the matter?"

"Nothing, Tolimra." He reached out to touch her hand reassuringly. "Go back to sleep." He lay down next to her, thinking wryly, *Maybe that's even true. I can't see what's out there yet. Maybe somebody fired it by mistake, or for a prank. Or maybe they're practicing.*

But Terek's mind could not long indulge in far-fetched possibilities conjured up solely to be comforting, and they quickly gave way to thoughts about what he knew beyond almost any doubt was really out there. That cannon shot had been fairly far off—probably the one up at the extreme east end of the island which Yldac and its farms now occupied. That fit the pattern—those who had taken the threat of Ketaxil raids as seriously as it deserved had always said they were most likely to come from that direction. The few skirmishes Yldac had already experienced gave some support to that theory. Single Ketaxil ships had raided a few farms on the island's edge, and without exception they had come from the east, suggesting that they still preferred to stick fairly close to the sea itself. So far no Ketaxil had managed to land in the town itself, but Terek suspected they hadn't really tried very hard. And the Templemen who had managed to bring those manuscripts and relics back from Ybhal had also brought rumors of worse things in store.

Oddly, even as Terek thought about those chilling rumors and how they might apply to the impending raid, the thoughts his dreams had stirred about the manuscripts kept writhing in his mind.

He must have done a poor job of concealing his agitation. After a few minutes, even though there had been no more obvious sounds of danger, Tolimra complained, "I can't go back to sleep. What were you looking at outside, Terek?"

Next to her, Dajhek stirred. In years he was no older than

Tolimra, but his body and mind wore the years more heavily. His skin was more wrinkled, the three webbed crests that were all that remained of his youthful mane dry and cracked, his breathing less dependable, his mind inclined to wander. "Something outside?" he muttered. "What's outside? Terek?"

"No, Dajhek," said Terek. "I'm here. I'm not sure what's outside." *But I'm afraid I will be, too soon,* he thought grimly. "Let me fix you some breakfast."

He got up and went to the fireplace. Silently, listening, he got the bellows and some starter pellets and fresh wood and set about building a new fire over last night's ashes. As it roared into life, the cannon at the east end of the island barked again, and another answered it from somewhere else. Terek started at the sound, and Tolimra sat suddenly upright, fear engraved on her face.

"Terek!" she gasped. "Those are cannons. The Ketaxil must be coming!" Dajhek, a sad shadow of his former self, mumbled something unintelligible.

"I'm afraid so," Terek sighed, resigned. "Rest. There's nothing we can do about it." Stubbornly determined to follow his own good advice, he concentrated fiercely on bringing the pot of gruel to a boil. But he couldn't really keep his mind off what was happening. Not with the increasingly frequent and close sounds of gunfire, and the growing chorus of slamming doors and excited conversation in the street outside.

And through it all, as if with perverse volition of their own, the dream-thoughts kept shouting louder and louder at him.

Suddenly, just as the gruel reached readiness, a cannon boomed very nearby and the talk outside swelled to shouts.

The atmosphere turned in an instant to one of imminent battle. Terek jerked the gruel off the fire, set it on the eating table, and started for the door in one swift, continuous motion. "I'm going to see what's going on out there," he muttered. "Your breakfast is ready."

He was already at the door. As he passed through and locked it, he barely heard Tolimra warn him, "Be careful!"

He hurried past the last row of shacks to get an unobstructed view of the waterfront. There he found a crowd of his neighbors jostling each other for better places at the very edge of land, jabbering excitedly and pointing out on the water. Terek noticed the two outlanders he had seen earlier, huddled against the side of a shack as if hoping to escape danger that way. He saw now that they were a man and a woman, neither very old, and though they flattened themselves against the wall as if trying to hide, they too were intently watching something on the water.

Terek gave them little notice, but followed their gaze. The fog had dissipated somewhat; its early morning smell was being crowded out by the acrid smoke of burnt gunpowder. Visibility on the water was not yet good, but Terek could easily make out the two flamboyantly carved and decorated Ketaxil ships far out on it. They seemed nearly stationary; one of them was in flames, with men swarming off it under a billowing column of black smoke and crossing to the other ship in a small boat.

And a third ship was closer than Terek had ever seen one before. He gasped when he saw it, astonished at the realization that he had missed it at first. Already it was little more than fifty or sixty yards offshore, and heading straight toward the crowd onshore at alarming speed under the combined power of well-trimmed sails and battle-mad oarsmen. The prow, carved in the image of some bloodthirsty monster which might or might not exist somewhere on Ymrek, towered higher and higher as it approached, scattering spray high into the air before it. Terek felt a transient surge of potential panic—something that tried to assert itself as certainty that he was about to be killed. Then he squelched that and his gaze flashed over the scene onshore, looking to see what was being done. That smell of gunpowder must have come from something nearby. . . .

A few yards to his right, a half-dozen half-trained Keldac soldiers, some of them with their hands full just keeping the crowd out of the way, were struggling to turn a wooden-wheeled antique cannon to aim at the approaching ship. Terek didn't recognize the gun—there had been no permanent installation here, so it must have just been wheeled here this morning—but the general design of both its barrel and its carriage was thoroughly familiar. The soldiers were working partly at cross-purposes, snarling instructions at each other while two armored Templemen tried to keep order by shouting directions from the saddles of two magnificent, shiny-antlered doral. Meanwhile the Ketaxil ship seemed to come faster and faster.

From somewhere amid the confusion came a loud, distinct command: *"Fire!"* Reaction was not quite instantaneous, but very shortly one of the soldiers touched a glowing torchlet to the fuse on top of the cannon's barrel. A crackling sound managed to make itself heard over everything else, lasting several seconds while the soldiers still struggled to follow the target with the cumbersome weapon.

Then it went off, with a roar nearly deafening at such close range and accompanied by a transient tongue of red flame that flicked from the barrel. The cannon, momentarily shrouded in smoke, shook and rolled jerkily back. The ball splashed into the water, well out and well away from the ship.

The ship sped on, now so close that there was no possible hope of reloading in time for another shot—yet the soldiers were trying to do it anyway. Terek groaned; in its way, the whole defense effort was almost comical. *It's a miracle*, he thought, *that we've done as well as we have so far.*

The ship had seemed on the verge of running right up onto the ground. Now, abruptly, it was changing course. Oars were dipped and held rigidly; hands on deck were changing the arrangement of sails. The ship was so close that Terek could easily hear, though not understand, the commands being shouted on board in the nasal singsong of Litaxil. Water churned violently around the hull as it wheeled as if to beat a hasty retreat to open water. That didn't make sense, but for an instant Terek almost dared hope that that was what was happening. The dora-mounted Templemen did, too, shrilly urging their soldiers to get their cannon ready while the ship was in a weak position.

Then Terek saw what was really happening. Ropes quickly but smoothly lowered a small boat from the ship's stern, and heavily armed crewmen swarmed down rope ladders into it. His eye just happened to catch the motion of one who had remained aboard the ship firing a crossbow. An incredibly short instant later, a scream just to his right sent a shivery shock through his whole being. He turned automatically, in time to see the soldier collapsing to the ground next to the cannon, blood spurting from both sides of his neck where the bolt had skewered it. Terek watched with an emotion he could not name, but some elements of it were not as strong as he would have expected. He had never seen a man killed before, at least since he was old enough to understand what he was seeing, and much of the reality hardly registered. Too much else was happening. He caught another motion near the cannon and saw one of the Templemen wheel and shout a curt command to his mount. The dora dashed off, its hooves pounding the street thunderously.

Out on the water, the ship had completed its wheeling maneuver and was speeding back out to follow its surviving companion toward the sea. But the little boat continued toward shore at a rapid clip, half a dozen men in the stern rowing with powerful, concerted rhythm while the half dozen toward the bow prepared their crossbows with obvious relish. Several Keldac on shore screamed and the crowd scattered. Some ran headlong toward the monastery; others, including Terek, sought shelter behind nearby shacks, risking greater personal danger so they could keep watching. The soldiers, and their one remaining commander, stuck to their posts and got off another shot from the cannon; it was a clear miss.

Just fifty feet from his own shack, Terek saw history enter a new and unwelcome phase. For the first time, Ketaxil raiders actually landed in Yldac. Their boat came almost to the rock retaining wall, and at the last possible second halted abruptly as one of the raiders threw an anchor overboard. Then they all came ashore, some in single leaps, others splashing through the shallow water, all making a racket well calculated to terrify. Terek had never before seen

Ketaxil at close range, and their appearance fully matched their reputation. They were tall, muscular men, darker-haired than Kengmorl, with wildly flowing full beards. At least Terek assumed they were all men, though he had heard that among the Ketaxil both sexes wore the beards and took part in warfare. In any case, they were formidable-looking and armed to the teeth, with leather-and-metal armor and both short and long swords in addition to their crossbows. As they hit the shore they scattered in all directions, shrieking wildly. None came directly toward Terek—yet—but he saw one shoot a neighbor girl in the leg and then, laughing uproariously, cut both her arms off with his long sword and leave her to lie there while he went looking for other amusement. At the sight of that cruelty, even though the stories had led him to expect it, Terek truly and thoroughly sickened. He felt a nearly overwhelming desire to do something for the girl, or at the very least stop the barbarian—but he knew there was nothing he could do, so he forced himself to simply tear his eyes away from her and stay flattened against the wall.

He heard the cannon fire once more; he couldn't see whether it hit anything. He heard the shrieks and moans of other Keldac victims mingle with the attacker's whoops. He saw crackling flames spring up from a shack near his own, and wondered with strange detachment what he was going to do when one of the barbarians found him here and decided it was his turn.

Then he heard hoofbeats and new shouts. The Templeman who had ridden off when the first soldier was shot had returned with six or seven others, all armored, mounted, and carrying bifurcated side lances that weren't the ceremonial kind. Their long weapons and tall, powerful animals gave them enough advantage so they could ride right into the Ketaxil, stabbing and trampling to put them out of action. Not with complete impunity, of course—the Templemen were still vulnerable to crossbow bolts aimed well and without delay, and at least two of them fell, one hurt seriously and the other slightly—but they were able to restore quiet within a few frenzied minutes. Quiet, that is, except for the flames of the burning shack and the muffled sounds of the injured in the streets. With the immediate threat over and the ships apparently leaving, the Templemen came down off their mounts and set about the slow, painful task of trying to help those victims they could.

The girl Terek had seen mutilated was not one of the first they reached. As soon as he was sure the danger was past, he hurried to her side to see if there was any chance he could help. But he could see none. She was not quite dead yet, but he was sure it would not be long. Consciousness had long since gone, so he couldn't even say anything to her. He had not known her well, but she was not a total stranger and she had seemed pleasant and bright—and even if she had been a stranger, he couldn't watch that happen to anybody without wanting to do something.

He stood up, all the emotion he had been too preoccupied to feel during the battle beginning to flow into him in an almost unbearable flood. He had heard of the Ketaxil before; he had even seen a few from a distance. He had heard of their delight in cruelty for cruelty's sake, tempered only by care to leave enough so they could profitably raid the same place again later. He had heard that, with the new waterways opened up by the Shakes, they presented a grave threat to the entire fabric of Yngmor's civilization; he had even been one of those who took the threat seriously—on an intellectual level. But even the most vivid intellectual awareness cannot compare with actual experience, and now, for the first time, he *felt* the reality of all those things at a level that pervaded his whole consciousness. For the first time, he felt as an immediate, personal reality the threat to his town, his life and work, his civilization itself.

And therefore he felt as a matter of urgent personal concern that *he* must do something to avert the danger. He wasn't sure what, yet, but he was startled to discover that even through the attack and its aftermath, the almost-thoughts about this morning's dream had never left his mind. They were still throbbing persistently there, and, if anything, growing rather than diminishing in intensity. He felt a sudden strong hunch that his subconscious was trying to tell him something—that, whatever else might be there, the manuscripts and his dreams somehow held a way to help.

And it was none to early to find out what it was. Forcing the recent violence to the back of his mind, pausing only to make sure his home and parents were safe, he hurried off to the monastery as his neighbor's shack continued to burn.

Terek was not the only witness who watched the battle with concern, nor was he the only one who wanted to help. As he returned to his work, the two robed outlanders he had noticed came out of their hiding place and started through the narrow streets—briskly, as if they had a definite destination and were in a hurry to get there. They went some distance before either of them spoke.

Then Chet Barlin said, "Well, now you've seen the problem firsthand. *I'm* convinced. We ought to try to help. How about you?"

"*Something* certainly needs to be done," Tina agreed. "But . . . do you have something in mind?"

"Nothing specific. But we'll have time to think about it—time to figure something out. We can't do anything like that without checking with headquarters first. And we have to check in person."

For an instant, Tina showed dismay; then it faded to something milder. "In person," she repeated. "It's such a long trip. . . ."

"True. Do you think it isn't worth it?"

She was silent for a few seconds. He watched her face, following her thoughts. Finally she said, "No. I don't want to have to watch anything like that very often. Especially not if I know it's partly my fault."

The decision was made. With no further discussion, they returned to their landing boat—which was, to say the least, rather different from that of the Ketaxil.

And, as Tina had said, it would be a long trip—for she and Chet were outlanders such as not even Terek had ever imagined.

2

Some two weeks and two dozen light-years went by before the landing boat once more detached itself from its parent craft to carry the Barlins "ashore." The starship hung in orbit, just high enough so they could see the planet below as a complete sphere as they started down. The boat fell gently and silently; Tina and Chet sat silently before a big viewing panel and watched the planet come up to meet them. Neither of them was subject to any overpowering emotions about "home," but a return to Larneg—a globe of marbled greens and golds and blues and whites on the day side and black velvet dotted here and there by glowing pinpoints of cities beyond the terminator—was always worth watching.

If you thought about Larneg's history, it was a little ironic that she was now not only the nucleus of the largest existing human political unit but also the most avid seeker of new Earthlike worlds. If you thought instead about the present face of the planet, it was almost hard to believe that it had all started as the first spectacular triumph of terraforming.

As the surface rose, ceased to be a sphere, and spilled beyond the limits of vision, the splashes of color resolved themselves into forests and fields and lakes. Stiv Sandor, the starship's copilot and chauffeur for landing parties, aimed the boat at a dot on the horizon and dipped the nose more steeply. The dot grew into a city. Details swelled to become buildings and streets and formal gardens, whizzing by until finally the boat slowed and settled gently onto a paved landing field. Automatic adjustments hummed and hissed for a minute; then all was silent and a door gaped open to bright sunshine and balmy air. Stiv remained with the boat, waiting to arrange long-term parking, while Chet and Tina released their seat belts and stepped out.

Moving strips carried them swiftly to the edge of the landing field. There the strips ended and they walked with light step on sandy paths across the broad garden surrounding the spaceport. Open, blue sky sprawled overhead; down here, green leaves and wildly colored flowers glistened in the white light of two blazing suns.

Less than twelve hundred years ago it had all been barren.

From Larneg, Capella A looked much like Sol seen from Earth; Capella B, close to it in the sky, was considerably smaller. A was a giant—Larneg was much farther from its whirling pair of suns than Earth was from Sol. Early explorers here had found a planet without life of its own—but in an orbit that could be hospitable to terrestrial life, once established, for millions of years to come. Terraforming enthusiasts had seized the challenge and in a few centuries succeeded beyond their wildest dreams. Since then, of course, terraforming had fallen into almost complete disuse as the abundance of "ready-made" worlds became evident.

At the outer edge of the park, an underground shuttle whisked the Barlins in minutes to the heart of the Capital. They emerged from the terminal into a forest of glittering towers, some of them rising two hundred feet toward the sky. Even here, scattered among the buildings, were neat ornamental plots of authentic Terran plants. And here the moving strips formed and intricate and crowded network, buzzing with the business of the Grand Republic.

The contrast to quiet, preindustrial, almost rural Yldac was striking. *And yet*, Chet reflected, *we were there once. Where might we be now, if things had been different?*

The term "Grand Republic of Larneg" might seem a bit presumptuous, from one point of view. True, its seventy worlds formed by far the largest federation of mankind, not only at the present time, but in recorded history. But the entire sphere of human colonization—and that included far more than the Grand Republic—was barely four hundred light-years across. And that was a mere speck out in the hinterlands of a galaxy a hundred thousand light-years across.

But there was one respect in which the Republic was undeniably grand: it had one of the most ornate bureaucracies that ever grew. That fact lay behind the necessity for a personal trip to the Capital in at least two ways. First was simply the legal requirement, imposed by an increasingly cautious and stodgy Bureau of Extraterrestrial Life, that *any* request for permission to intervene in an alien culture be justified in a personal appearance. That was to discourage such requests from being made lightly.

And secondly, it was too much to expect that any action could be obtained without a ritual runaround of at least half a dozen offices. Since human interstellar communication still depended on automatic Kokes-tunneling message capsules being sent bodily from one spacebound communication station to another, trying to conduct that kind of business from the frontier could take forever—and be prohibitively expensive. It was cheaper to go to Larneg.

In Chet and Tina's case, the runaround included eight offices. Three days after planetfall, they sat in the outer office of Tomas Flangan, comforted only by the realization that if anything was going to be settled, it would have to be here. Flangan was *the* Secretary of Extraterrestrial Life. There was no higher they could go in this branch of the government.

They were ushered in after a half-hour wait. Flangan was a smallish, elderly man, bald except for a white fringe around the back of his head, who gave an instant impression of fussiness. He wore the high-collared, sleeveless costume currently *de rigueur* among both sexes in the Capital, and somehow managed to make it look even more uncomfortable than it felt. His head bobbed slightly atop the stiff collar as he glanced up at Chet and Tina, grunted absently, and motioned them to a pair of deep leather chairs. Then his eyes dropped back to the packet of papers on the antique ebony desk. Chet had no idea just how old the furniture was, but he was pretty sure it was the same he had seen in pictures of Bernard Mauricio, who left this office almost a century earlier.

Flangan's features formed an odd, mild frown, half puzzled, half annoyed. He shuffled back and forth through the papers for a while without saying anything. Finally he said, a bit petulantly and still without looking up, "I don't really understand why you're here. I mean, why wasn't this matter settled by my subordinates? Why did it have to come all the way to me?"

"I suppose," said Chet, "they saw enough merit in our request to make them afraid to turn it down. But they thought you should be the one to give final approval."

"Hmph." Flangan stared silently at the top page while he got a plug of chew from a carved silver box and put it in his mouth. He closed the box without offering the Barlins any, chewed meditatively for a few seconds, and finally looked squarely at Chet. "You want to intervene in an alien culture, eh? Why?"

"Because," said Chet, "we think it's necessary. Are you pretty familiar with the situation from the documents you have there?"

"They're clear as mud. You give me a quick rundown."

"All right. Ymrek is a terrestroid planet with humanoid natives. Tina and I were there with a cultural study party. Perfectly routine, at the start, but some less routine things have come up. The planet is far from unified; the most advanced cultures could be called barbarian and feudal types. There's a lot of diversity. Several groups travel, and yet no one culture knows very much about the whole planet—which was very convenient for us. We learned enough from our preliminary studies with Maksutov scopes and parabolic mikes and PFSUs to let us go in for a closer look at a couple of cultures by disguising ourselves as travelers from other parts of the planet. Very quiet, unobtrusive travelers—but the point is, we were able to pass ourselves off as Kemrekl."

"Kemrekl?"

"Name for the natives, in one language," Tina explained.

"An agglutinative language, basically. Class prefix, root, plural suffix."

"Oh." Flangan looked back to Chet. "So you passed yourselves as natives, eh? I take it they must be *quite* humanoid."

"They are. Some of the most humanoid we've ever found. There've only been one or two other cases where a survey party would have dared try this." He chuckled. "We couldn't have got away with it if they'd been thoroughgoing nudists, but luckily most of them aren't."

"I see," said Flangan. "I'm afraid I still don't see what there is in all this to make you want to tamper."

"One of those cultures is special. I mentioned that there are many native cultures and we spot-sampled several. We saw one and only one with something definitely beyond barbarism. A place with a notable resemblance to medieval Europe, if you remember your Terran history. A place, in fact, that seemed to be right on the brink of a flowering something like the Renaissance that was so important to the beginning of pre-modern civilization."

"Good for them," Flangan grunted, turning to spit toward a cuspidor on his side of the desk. "So what?"

"So that flowering probably isn't going to happen unless we help."

Flangan's eyebrows rose slightly and then his eyes narrowed. "Oh? Maybe you'd better explain that."

Chet nodded. "The place I'm talking about is a peninsula called Yngmor—except that it isn't a peninsula anymore. It apparently had a long record of minor earthquakes, but a few years ago it had a dilly. Shook the peninsula right apart—shattered it into a bunch of islands with a network of waterways among them."

Flangan shrugged. "So let them build boats. If you're going to cite Terran history to me, how about a place called Venice?"

Chet shook his head. "Not the same situation. Venice was one city. Yngmor is a lot of separate small towns—especially separate since the quake. Some of the towns were destroyed completely; others badly damaged; some are still reasonably intact but isolated and short on food. And vulnerable."

"Vulnerable?"

"To the Ketaxil. A seafaring barbarian tribe from the mainland coast east of Yngmor who live by raiding coastal towns. There were enough victims on the coasts so they never had to venture inland very much. For just that reason, many Kengmor towns were well inland. But now they're not. And they're as unused to water fighting as the Ketaxil are to land fighting. The Ketaxil are catching on."

"Is that necessarily bad? Adversity is character-building, they tell me. These raiders ought to provide a stimulus. I'd think they might speed up the development of your budding civilization."

"Agreed, up to a point. But it's only a beneficial stimulus if the Kengmorl have a fighting chance of reacting fast enough to save themselves. As it is, that chance is very slim. The Ketaxil are too overwhelming—they're likely to stimulate Yngmor right to death. They've already ransacked several monasteries that the Shakes missed, and virtually paralyzed communications among the survivors."

Flangan fished a paper out of the middle of his packet and stared at it. "Hmph," he said finally. "I'm not sure I find your evaluation convincing, but for the moment let's suppose it's right. It says here that what you propose to do about it is to introduce a few Reynolds airfloaters with Type 76CB3 Quasimaterial control elements. That's all?"

Chet nodded. "Yes."

"That's plenty. How in the world do you expect to take something like that into a feudal culture without giving yourselves away?"

"It's right there in the report," Chet reminded him, " 'By skillfully disguising them as imports from a remote region of the planet, it is believed that they can restore an adequate level of communication with a minimum of disturbance and without arousing suspicions of their true nature and origin.' "

"You *have* to be kidding," Flangan muttered, shaking his head. "I'm sorry, but I can't see this doing anything to justify such playing with fire. I don't see how I can approve it."

Chet winced. That sounded like final disapproval; now he and Tina would have to try to change Flangan's mind. He glanced at Tina to gauge her reaction, but her head was turned so her long blond hair hid her face.

Chet forced himself to resist opening his mouth until he had paused to think it over. He reflected with a sense of irony on how much the Bureau of Extraterrestrial Life had changed in a hundred years. Then blatant Expansionists had shrilly urged the Republic on to colonize every habitable planet it found, even if a native race had to perish in the process—as several did. That trend had culminated in Bernard Mauricio's scandalous attempt to institutionalize routine genocide in the name of humanity. Mauricio had been thwarted by the strange uprising of colonists on a backwoods planet called Lorania—but that had in turn started the pendulum swing to the bureau's present pussyfooting reluctance to even touch an alien culture. Moderation—rationality—in public affairs seemed to exist (when at all) only as a brief transient on the way from one extreme to another.

"Do you remember," Chet asked quietly, "the bureau's basic policy statement?" He stopped short of pointing out that a framed wall copy was plainly visible over Flangan's shoulder, but he read part of one of the goals listed there. "'. . . to observe other cultures, to learn, to protect from human injustice, to give help where it is needed . . .'" He looked squarely at Flangan. "Isn't it odd that that's hardly ever been done?"

Flangan glared at him. "The reason is the part right after what you chose to rip out of its context. It says 'to give help *without interfering with the culture's own development.*' How do you decide when you're doing one without the other?"

"You think about it very carefully," said Chet. "You don't just decide arbitrarily that everything you might do is automatically and *a priori* bad and so never do anything. Not if you really care about what you do. I guess you might define it so that you're interfering any time you touch—but then maybe sometimes interference is better." He saw from Flangan's face that that line of argument wasn't working. He smiled diplomatically, to soften it, and tried again. "Look, Mr. Flangan, don't think we'd ask for this on a casual whim. We have plenty of reservations about it. In my profession, I've had plenty of chance to see the damage something like this can do. I'd never suggest it unless I thought the case was very exceptional. But I think this case *is* very exceptional. Let me put it bluntly—but without exaggeration. If we don't do anything, the most promising culture on Ymrek *is* going to be wiped out. All we ask is to add one small thing to give them a slight added chance to help themselves."

"Hmph." Flangan's face was still hard, but for the first time Chet thought he saw signs of weakening. And he could see now that Tina thought she saw them, too. The Secretary said, "And just how do you propose to see that that's *all* that happens? Quasimaterials are new and strange even to us. What kind of superstitious reactions might *they* have?"

"Less than you'd expect, we think," said Tina. "As Chet said earlier, we think we can pass them off as imports from another part of the planet and—"

"Bah!" Flangan exploded. "Do you seriously expect me to buy that? How could anybody there make anything like that? It takes a level of technology vastly beyond anything they—"

"*You* know that," Tina interrupted, "but *they* don't. You're looking at the whole thing from a Larnegite's point of view; they'll see it from a Kengmor's, which is entirely different. There are several things in our favor. The Kengmorl are stay-at-homes. They haven't seen much of the planet. But they have seen a fair variety of exotic imports brought by travelers from cultures that are more inclined to roam, and for all they know, practically anything could exist out there. Quite a few of the wanderers put on magic shows and the Kengmorl eat them up. And they don't assume it's just sleight of hand—they believe they're seeing just what it looks like, and it doesn't faze them. I'm not going to try to explain their religion to you in a few words—though you'll find a fair summary among your papers—but I will remind you of one of its three basic tenets. It says: 'Magnificent and infinitely varied are the ways of the Supreme Presence.' They really believe that, in a way that'll take you a while to grasp. They're at least as casual about accepting the unfamiliar as any group we've ever met. We think we can slip a few quasimaterial-controlled floaters in with hardly a ripple."

"You *think*," Flangan scowled. "But how are you going to *know*, before it's too late?"

Tina almost giggled, but resisted in time. "Why, we'll do some preliminary studies, of course. We'll very carefully expose them to small samples of quasimaterials of various types and see how they react to their unusual behavior."

"How?"

"We'll be magicians." Flangan's eyebrows rose slightly and Tina explained, "I told you about the magic shows. We'll pose as a band of foreigners who go around giving them. And our magic will just happen to include quasimaterials."

"Hm-m-m." Flangan looked for one of his papers, studying it, and remarked, "It says here the two of you specifically ask to lead this party personally. Why?"

"Simply because we think we have special qualifications for it that nobody else does at present," said Tina. "As a team. Chet's a comparative historian; I'm a xenologist. And we both already have at least as much inside familiarity with Ymrek as anybody else."

"Hm-m-m." Flangan stared at his documents a little longer. Then he snapped the packet shut and said, "I'll have to think it over. I'll call you in the morning."

It was actually midafternoon before the viewphone in the Barlin's hotel room chimed. They both, having been there all morning, waiting, hurried to the communications nook. Chet pressed a button and a lifelike bust of Flangan appeared on the platform, looking out at them with a flat expression. "I've decided to grant your request," he said grudgingly. "On two conditions."

He paused as if waiting for comment. Finally Chet said only, "Yes?"

"First," said Flangan, "your party will include a representative of Quasimaterials, Incorporated. His function will be to supervise production of any quasimaterials you use and to advise on alternatives if any must be considered."

Chet nodded slightly. "And the other?"

"Your party will also include a BEL field agent, handpicked by me, with full veto power on anything you propose. In case anything goes wrong."

Chet pressed his lips together in disgust. The crippling potential of the second condition was obvious—but he judged that the deal was the best he could hope for at present. They would have to settle for it. "I can accept that," he said coolly. "*If* anything goes wrong, which we most definitely plan to avoid."

"The best-laid plans . . ." Flangan muttered. "I really hope you're right. I still don't like this business. I'm afraid we're all going to be sorry you meddled. You just wait and see if I'm not right."

3

Terek paused, when his eyes grew too weary of close work, to let himself drink in the flavor of the day. It was the first in the three weeks since his dream—and the Ketaxil landing—when he had not been overwhelmed with tasks set to him by Ravilyr and the others. He had devoted every available minute, including working far into the night by candlelight at home, to following up the dream. But the minutes had been too few. So today, when Ravilyr had smiled genially and said he had nothing in particular for Terek to do, Terek had seized the chance to take his notebooks and go and hide among the ash trees on the monastery's second terrace.

The second terrace was one of his favorite spots. The monastery, of course, dominated the town, rising from its center in an imposing series of such expansive stone tiers, surmounted finally by the spires and minarets of the central castle. Only the top of the second tier was so lavishly planted with trees and gardens, offering a blend of shade, sun, and solitude that was nearly ideal for study and contemplation. And when, as now, the need for a break made itself felt, he had a choice of views. He could look out over the periphery, with wisps of smoke curling up from the bulbous tops of thin chimneys, and beyond at the surrounding plain, dotted with tiny farmhouses and bordered by water and thickets. Or he could look up at the walls and towers leading his gaze steeply and inevitably to the crowning chamber where the dixar himself lived and ruled.

Today he preferred the periphery and the plain, for it was there that he could see the season beginning to change.

The wisps from the chimneys, more prevalent than a few weeks ago, merged almost imperceptibly with a faint smoky haze that lay lightly over the whole landscape. Black and silver had already begun to tip the leaves of the ash trees here on the terrace and in the thicket to the west. The full somber glory of fall was not far off.

Terek moved to the very edge for a better look at the thicket. *But only for a few minutes,* he cautioned himself. *I'm too close to start loafing. . . .* He leaned against one of the globe-surmounted columns which rimmed this level, their bases merging into inverted arches which were pleasant to see from the streets below and even more pleasant to stretch out against in a sunny spot on a cool day. He looked off and tried to think idly of what might lie hidden in the thicket. He had been into it, once when he was very young, but he remembered little, and few Keldacl ever bothered to go there. Even firewood gathered there was too poor to bother with, if anything better was available. *Someday*, Terek thought lazily, *I'm going back. Maybe I'll see something there that everybody else missed. It wouldn't be the first time. . . .*

And that thought put an end to his brief attempt at idleness, because it reminded him once again of his work and where it seemed to be leading. He reached out, pulled his notebook to where he was sitting, and reopened it to where he'd been working when his eyes got tired. He'd copied the key numbers from the Ybhal manuscripts and he'd almost finished his painstaking drawing. It looked so good that when he thought about it he couldn't wait to see if the pattern actually persisted until the end. He picked up his quill and ink and straightedge and protractor and carefully—*most* carefully—measured off the last two dozen data from the manuscripts. With each successive dot he drew, his pulse seemed to speed up a little. Before the last one, he held his breath and hesitated as if afraid it would fall in the wrong place and ruin everything.

But it didn't. With unerring, uncanny precision it fell right where Terek's intuition had told him it would two days ago. Trembling, he double-checked the distance and angle he had measured, and triumphantly drew the dot in bold ink.

And then he completed the last circle.

He stared at it for half a minute, both proud and awed. Then he let the notebook drop to his lap while he leaned his head back against the warm stone and closed his eyes as if exhausted.

A familiar voice drifted up from the courtyard far below. Terek opened his eyes to see two Templemen, in loose robes of the same olive brown fabric as his own Disciple's suit, strolling the cobblestones. One of them he didn't know, but the other he knew as well as anyone in the world. "Ravi!" he called out, standing up excitedly and waving. "Up here!"

The two Templemen stopped and turned together to look up at him. The one Terek didn't know frowned slightly, presumably at Terek's addressing his companion by name. Ravilyr was the only Templeman Terek would address so, but that he did not only without qualms but with pride. Ravilyr was his tutor and Terek was Ravilyr's favorite Disciple, and that relationship was close enough to give him the right. Not the right to use his *whole* name, to be sure, but even just "Ravi" was quite an honor.

Ravi looked up with a kindly smile. "Yes, Terek? What are you doing up there?"

"Thinking," said Terek. "I've got something to show you. When can you look at it?

Ravi looked at him for a few seconds as if trying to evaluate his protégé's enthusiasm. Then he exchanged a few unheard words with the other Templeman and called up, "I'll be right there, Terek." The other Templeman walked slowly on, alone, while Ravi disappeared into a door in the wall below Terek.

Moments later, he reappeared on this level, stepping out of an arched black doorway and wending his silent way among the ash trees to the spot where Terek again sat. Terek started to rise respectfully, but Ravi motioned him back. "No need," he chuckled. "Stay where you are. I'll join you." He did so, gathering his robe to one side so he could sit facing Terek from the next pillar, resting easily with his back against the stone and one foot dangling over the edge. Ravi was starting to show his age, physically—the three crests were beginning to show through his pale orange mane, and his skin was less smooth than a few years ago—but there was a certain youthfulness in his outlook that he seemed unlikely ever to lose.

His eyes sparkled as he looked at Terek and the papers he had gathered around him. "Well, my boy. What's up?"

"My spirits," Terek grinned. "You remember the manuscripts you turned over to me for cataloging? The ones that were saved from the monastery at Ybhal after the Ketaxil wiped it out?"

"Yes." Ravi's face grew momentarily solemn as he remembered the tragedy. And the bravery of the Keldac Templemen who had finally succeeded in salvaging a few documents and relics by taking a dugout there at night, running without lights and hugging the shore. "What about them?"

"I've been reading them. There are a couple of interesting items among them. Items which may be important."

"Oh?"

"Yes. Let me show you. Here's one." Terek riffled through the papers until he found the group of yellowing pages on falling bodies. Page after page, they were, of sketches and rows of numbers. He thrust them eagerly at Ravi.

Ravi took them and looked through several pages. He didn't quite seem to understand. Finally he asked, "What are they?"

"Notes on the way things fall. *Quantitative* notes, with numbers telling just how fast they fall. All kinds of things, dropped from different heights. Some Templeman put a lot of effort into devising ways to actually measure these things. And then he did it, and wrote down all the numbers." Terek watched Ravi's face expectantly, but still it showed little sign of appreciation. If there was any expression at all there, it was the merest suggestion of a puzzled frown. Disappointed, Terek finished, "There seems to be a pattern in them."

"Oh." Ravi let his eyes linger a few more seconds on the papers, then looked up at Terek with a brighter expression.

"And what else did you find?"

"These." Terek stuffed the falling-body papers back into their places and pulled out the others. "Somebody else's notes on the Wandering Stars," Terek explained, handing them to Ravi.

"Ah." Ravi's face brightened as he took them. These he could recognize at once, and appreciate. Every Templeman knew well the current pattern of motion of the Wanderers, and the way it related to the Covenant from Before Time. Approvingly, he traced out one of the diagrams, showing Ymrek plainly labeled at the center with the Day Star and each Wandering Star moving in a path which could be analyzed into a system of circles, the center of each circle moving along a larger circle. "Some of the original work on epicycles, no doubt," said Ravi. "And yet I don't recognize this hand"—he flipped to the front of the sheaf, looked for something, found it—"or the author's name." He glanced through the other pages, slowing variants on the theme, enlarged details, and columns of venerable numbers giving observed positions of the Wandering Stars. "Excellent," he said finally, beaming. "The Archivist will be proud of you, Terek. *I* am proud of you."

"Thank you, Ravi." Terek averted his gaze slightly and tried to brace his nerve. The important part he would tell no one but Ravi, and he was slightly apprehensive about even his tutor's reaction to it. But it had to be done. "These aren't the part I most wanted to show you," he said. "Certainly they are of historical value, but little more. The description of motions itself is just repetition of well-established Temple doctrine. Only the source is new. But look at this." Half eager, half fearful, he turned to the page with the strange inscription. "Here," he said, pointing it out with a fingertip. "Tiny, as if the writer almost hoped it wouldn't be seen, and yet had to write it. In a hand so cramped and distorted I can't tell whether it was the same man trying to disguise his writing, or somebody else who read these notes and got an idea. Read it."

The penmanship was so bad that Ravi had to hold the page close and squint to make it out. "'What if . . . '" He frowned. "'What if Ymrek weren't at the center?'" He read it again, then handed the paper back to Terek, frowning more deeply. "I don't understand. What else could *possibly* be at the center?"

"Just what I asked myself," said Terek, with the Kemrek version of a broad grin. "The writer didn't follow it up. That sentence is the only one in the book in that handwriting. But his question has been haunting me for the last three weeks. I kept wondering why he wrote it there. Was he really onto something? And why did he write it as if he was afraid to have it read?"

"Obviously," said Ravi, "because he *was* afraid to have it read. What could be plainer heresy? The Covenant from Before Time assures us that Ymrek is at the center of the universe, an unchanging focal point for all events. And that it always has been and always will be."

"Could it be that we've somehow *misunderstood* the Covenant?" Seeing the confused shock in Ravi's face, Terek hurried on, with growing apprehension, "Please, Ravi, hear me out. I just wondered why some old Templeman at Ybhal had even had that thought. Surely it couldn't hurt to think about how else things *might* have been, could it? If they actually weren't, thinking about them could only strengthen my understanding of how they actually are and thus my insight in the Ways. And isn't that what we're all striving for, ultimately? So I asked myself the same question you asked. What else could be at the center? And I tried to see what answers there might be, and what was wrong with them."

"I see," Ravi said cautiously. "And did you find answers?"

"Yes," said Terek. "One. But I haven't been able to find anything wrong with it."

For a moment Ravilyr looked stunned. He studied Terek's face for a while and then said quietly, "Perhaps I can help. What is this troublesome answer?"

"Suppose," said Terek, "the *Day Star* was at the center."

Ravi was silent for a long time. Then he laughed pleasantly. "Well, I think we can dispose of that easily enough.

I suppose you mean that Ymrek goes around the Day Star rather than vice versa?"

"Yes."

"Well, if that were the case, you could easily account for the Day Star's apparent daily motion. But why don't we *feel* the motion if we're moving? If you ride in a dora wagon, things are jostled all over. And yet we're not, on Ymrek." He chuckled. "Except during the Shakes, of course. But that's a different matter."

"Perhaps," Terek ventured, hoping he didn't sound sarcastic, "Ymrek is not bouncing along a cobblestone street like a dora wagon. They tell me that in a boat on smooth water you can close your eyes and forget you're moving. If Ymrek's motion around the Day Star were smooth enough, we might not notice it. For a moment, Ravi, just suppose that's how things are and think about the consequences. Let me show you what happened when I did that."

He brought his own notebook to the top of the pile and opened it to the figure he had completed just minutes earlier. "We have complete records of actual positions of the Wandering Stars and the Day Star—the same ones that were used to make the Ybhal drawings you were just looking at. I've used them a little differently. I started by assuming Ymrek describes an annual circle around the Day Star, meanwhile rotating. Then I marked off successive positions of the various Wandering Stars as seen from Ymrek and came up with this scheme." He passed it to Ravi, pointing at the "bull's-eye" of the targetlike pattern. "By taking into account the periods, I've been able to account for all the detailed motions that have been seen through the centuries. Not perfectly, but very close. I think I can fix the few little discrepancies that remain by making slight modifications of some of the circles. But only little ones. The essential picture will stay the same. And you can see it's much simpler then the traditional view."

"Yes, I see." Ravi stared intently at the drawing, with obvious fascination—but not yet quite approval. He seemed oddly reluctant to commit himself. "This is extremely interesting, Terek. But let me offer you one word of caution.

Don't let yourself start feeling too confident that you're onto anything really big or final. Or even right."

Disappointment again thudded dully into Terek's consciousness. "You're not impressed?"

Ravi smiled gently. "I didn't say that. I'm just cautious, and I merely suggest that you be so, too—lest you be vulnerable. But I certainly must admit that at the very least you've happened onto an odd set of coincidences. It warrants further examination. May I borrow your notes for a while, Terek—to study them more closely?"

"Certainly."

"Thank you. I'll try to look them over and get back to you as soon as possible. Now, I'm afraid I must be off to an audience." He stood up, cradling Terek's papers in his arms, and lifted a free finger to wave a parting gesture. "Until."

He strolled through the trees toward the doorway from which he had emerged. Halfway there, he stopped and turned. "Oh, Terek. There was one more point that almost slipped my mind. I'd hoped it would become clear when you showed me the rest, but it didn't. What did that first set of numbers have to do with it?"

"The falling bodies?" Terek smiled self-consciously, apologetically. "I really don't know. So far I have only a hunch that they have anything at all to do with it. But I definitely have a hunch. I have a hunch."

"Oh." Terek watched his tutor turn and disappear into the gaping door without another word.

As Ravilyr carried the books along the long, torchlit corridor, with sunlight streaming in through an open door or window here and there, he turned his conversation with Terek over in his mind. He simply didn't know what to make of it. It was undoubtedly the strangest conversation they had ever had—but it was sometimes hard to distinguish strangeness from inspiration, if you stood too close. And Terek had long shown the potential for inspiration. . . .

Seeking understanding, Ravilyr let his mind wander nostalgically back through his years of increasingly close association with his Disciple. Terek has been a small boy—a very small boy—when it started. Merely one of the offspring of two of the flock who came to Ravilyr's chapel, in the northwest corner of the monastery, every time their Temple Morning rolled around. But those two had been so proud of their son—and rightly so—that they had been unable to resist bringing his talents to the attention of their Templeman. And the drawings they had showed him—sensitive renderings of the flowers that grew around their shack, done with color sticks from Tolimra's candlemaking supplies—had indeed been good. So good, in fact, that Ravilyr had immediately thought of the boy as a potential Fledgling.

He had not mentioned that in so many words to Dajhek and Tolimra, of course. But he had urged them to send Terek to study at the monastery. They had been pleased, but reluctant to part with him for more than day lessons. And about even that, the boy himself had had strong ideas—he wanted no part of any tutor but Ravilyr. Ravilyr had laughed good-naturedly at that, and tried to talk Terek out of his stubbornness—but not too hard, for in fact he was secretly flattered, and more than pleased to take Terek on as his own personal student.

He had remained pleased through all the years since, as Terek came every day to the monastery to discuss anything and everything with Ravilyr, and Ravilyr watched him grow steadily in knowledge and perceptiveness and curiosity and imagination.

And today?

Well, it was not inconceivable, Ravilyr admitted with a private smile, that his pupil had simply outdistanced him. And that did not seem by any means a bad thing.

He felt good about it as he stopped by his own chamber to drop the books off. He thought about it as he went through the motions of that silly routine audience that had been scheduled without consulting him. And then he returned to his chamber for that closer look at what Terek had done.

In every detail, the work was good. Terek was meticulous; he stated exactly what he was doing, and then did it expertly. If he made an assumption, he plainly labeled it as such. And by a carefully crafted succession of such steps, he had constructed a new picture of the universe—a picture that was simpler than the one Ravilyr had grown up with, and yet contradicted none of its actual observations.

Of course, there was something about the totality of the work which still dimly bothered Ravilyr. At first glance, it did seem to contradict Temple teachings. But would the dixar Kangyr actually consider it heretical? Ravilyr was not really sure—he had always thought of himself as a good but simple man with more understanding of the realities of life than of the subtleties of Temple doctrine—but he found it had to believe. What Terek had done was just too *good* for such an ignoble fate! Surely the dixar would recognize that it was simply an easier way of looking at what the Temple had known all along. . . .

In the end he decided that the imagination to see the easier way was evidence of such promise that he could not keep silent about it. He would have to mention it to the dixar.

He went the next morning. By the time he reached the top of the stairs, at the very apex of the church, he had to pause at the beginning of the last short corridor to regather his composure. He had not had personal audience with the dixar as much as half a dozen times previously in his entire life. When he did, he always felt uncomfortable and awed in the dixar's presence—craving that presence because of its holiness, and yet afraid that what he had to say would seem unimportant.

It happened this time as always. At length he felt bold enough to introduce himself to the young Templeman guarding the big wooden door, and the young Templeman went in to announce him. A moment later he was being ushered in, and the young Templeman went out and closed the door behind him.

Ravilyr was alone with the dixar Kangyr.

He gulped, overwhelmed by the magnificence of it all. "Your Holiness," he managed to say, and then his eyes flitted wildly around the chamber as a part of him automatically went through the elaborate salute to the dixar. He was distantly aware, and strangely thrilled, that the dixar returned it.

Then the dixar asked him to state his business. Ravilyr must have tripped over his tongue a dozen times, it seemed to him, before he finished describing the latest evidence of his brightest student's uniqueness. But finally it was all out—the whole tale of the Ybhal manuscripts, and the scrawled marginal note that started Terek thinking, and the way he had derived a simpler picture of the motions of everything by supposing that the Day Star was at the center and Ymrek circled it. Breathlessly, Ravilyr waited for the dixar's reaction.

The dixar Kangyr frowned. And that surprised and puzzled Ravilyr, for he had never seen the dixar frown before.

"Interesting," said the dixar Kangyr. "You must tell me more. And keep me posted."

4

The trip back to Ymrek gave time for Flangan's pessimism to recede into the backs of their minds, but from time to time Chet's kept reminding him that cultural tampering, no matter how well intentioned, *is* risky business. The thought was particularly strong when pilot Ben Jonz announced parking orbit maneuvers over the P.A. and Chet went into the lounge to watch.

He leaned back in one of the deep-cushioned reclining chairs and let his eyes focus on the big viewing panel that slanted between wall and ceiling. At first glance, the planet hanging in the blackness reminded him of Larneg under similar conditions—a similarly marbled globe of roughly similar colors. But there were differences. *Never forget that each world is unique, no matter how great the superficial similarities.* Even from here he could see differences, if he looked carefully. The average color of the vegetation was perceptibly different; in particular, the northern temperate regions, where fall was beginning, were flecked with a silvery sheen unique among all the planets Chet had visited. And the crescent of night that he could see from here lacked the conspicuous specks of bright cities . . .

His reverie was interrupted by the arrival of Bydron Kel, the field agent Tomas Flangan had handpicked to have final say on whether Project Airfloat would be carried through. He flopped his thin frame down in the next chair and looked indifferently at the screen while puffing on a cigarette. "Hi," he said, trying to be friendly. "One terrestroid looks pretty much like another, huh?"

"Only if you don't look close enough." Chet had found

it impossible to warm toward this young bureaucrat, even though it would have been good politics to do so. His first impression on meeting him had been, *He* looks *like somebody Flangan would handpick!* Not a young Flangan himself, exactly, but there was a definite family resemblance. Even out here, he kept his face smooth and wore the stiff-necked clothes of the Capital while everybody else was in casual field attire. And he seemed somehow to rub Chet the wrong way every time he opened his mouth.Part of it was undoubtedly due to real personality differences. But part of it, Chet admitted in a sudden moment of mellowness, was just as undoubtedly due to his own resentment of Kel's presence and function. He would have felt that no matter whom Flangan had sent. It was hardly fair to take it out on Kel personally—he might even turn out to be a decent sort when the chips were down, given a chance. Chet said more amicably, "I mean, sure there are a lot of similarities, at first glance. All really Earthlike planets have landmasses and oceans and clouds. But if you're going to stay in this kind of work, Bydron, you have to cultivate sensitivity to individual characteristics and differences, even if they seem small—"

"Excuse me," Kel interrupted stiffly, "but if you don't mind, I'd prefer to be called Agent Kel."

Chet broke off, not bothering to finish his sentence. At that moment Stiv Sandor stuck his head in the door. "Tallyho, folks!" he said cheerfully. "Preliminary parking maneuvers are completed. We're ready to board the boat and go down."

They followed Stiv out of the lounge. Chet was a little grateful for the interruption, and as they walked out he couldn't help thinking of the contrast between Kel and Stiv. Like terrestroid planets, they were superficially rather similar in appearance—and quite different in detail. The copilot also was clean-shaven and relatively young and thin, but his dress and air were as easy as those of anyone aboard. Chet had liked him from the start. (But then, he thought with a touch of self-reproach, how much of that was because Stiv was doing a job he could respect?)

It was hard to tell, in the crowded bay, but the landing boat had changed a good deal since its last visit here. Now, thanks to a new outer hull added on its recent visit to Larneg, it was invisible from the outside. That fact could be crucial, on a trip involving several prolonged stops near native towns. And the suggestion of the quasimaterial which made it possible, so new Chet had not yet heard of it, they owed entirely to Jem Wadkinz, the man from Quasimaterials, Inc.

Jem, as affable, slightly elfin fellow of middle years, with a conveniently blond beard, was already waiting at the open bay hatch. Just beyond it was the open hatch of the boat itself, showing the neatly furnished interior of the fore cabin—weirdly framed by an unobstructed view of the far side of the apparently empty bay. "Guess this is it," Jem grinned, nodding proudly at the boat. "Most unusual assignment anybody *I* know's been on for the company, I dare say. I'm looking forward to it—I think."

A latch clicked and Tina stepped into the boarding area. "I see the gang's all here," she smiled. "Hope I didn't keep you waiting."

The five of them filed aboard, Stiv going last to make sure the portal was secure. Then he took the pilot's seat that stood by itself in front of the main console, which curved around the rounded nose of the boat. The others strapped themselves into the row of seats behind Stiv's, facing forward so they could all see the viewing panel above the console. Stiv said something to his communicator and got an equally quiet and unintelligible reply from Ben. Then the boat fell free and the ship's pseudo-grav was felt no more. The viewing panel showed the bay yawning open and then, for just an instant, the ship jerking out of sight above as the planet started up.

Despite his harsh words to Kel, Chet could not help being impressed by how similar Ymrek and Larneg looked at this stage of the approach. But as they got closer and detail began to emerge from the general swirl of colors, the differences became more apparent. Not to Kel, perhaps, but definitely to Chet and Tina, who had been here before so that much was familiar. Yet even for them it was a new experience, because they were arriving at a new season, and the closer they got, the more evident the subtle transfiguration grew.

By the time Stiv zeroed in on their target area, it must have been quite apparent to Kel that they were far from Larneg. The monastery of Yxyngar, a typical stone wedding cake, loomed just ahead, and water glistened below. Stiv took the boat into a circle, pivoting around the monastery. "Looking for a landing site," he explained. "Last time here we used an abandoned farm, well away from the town proper. Looks like it's not quite so abandoned anymore."

He turned a knob and a luminous arrow appeared, pointing at a spot on the viewing panel. Magnification grew smoothly until their former landing site filled most of the screen. Some of the brush had been cleared away, and part of one field had been plowed.

Chet nodded. "Not surprising. With the isolation and the Ketaxil raids, they have food-supply problems. One partial solution is to plant fields they haven't been using. And we were already pretty sure they had some crops that like to be planted before winter."

"I wonder," Tina remarked, "if they've noticed any evidence of our being here before.'

"I doubt it," Stiv said. "We were pretty careful."

Chet noticed, with mild amusement, the expression on Kel's face. The BEL field agent had just begun to see the Yngmor situation as reality rather then mere words on paper—and his smugness seemed to be suffering a bit. He asked nervously, "Aren't they likely to hear the boat?"

Stiv shrugged. "It's pretty quiet. Landing boats are usually pretty quiet, and they're extra careful with the ones for survey parties." He had rolled the magnification back to normal; now he was zooming in on another spot. "Think I've found one. The land's actually a bit rolling over here, and I think there's a hole we can squeeze into among the trees in that hollow. Let's give it a try."

He dipped rather abruptly; for a moment it looked as if they would crash into the treetops. Then he paused, hovered, and lowered them straight down into a tight spot in a field too open to be called woods and two woodsy to be called open. Motion ceased; a minute later, so did the sounds. As Stiv had said, the boat was so quiet its operating noises were hardly noticed but their sudden cessation left a surprisingly gaping void.

"We're here," he announced. "I'll keep the meter running."

Tina and Chet, and then Jem and Kel, unbuckled and stood up. But this time the main hatch didn't open and they made no move to go outside. Instead they—except Kel—headed aft to their staterooms to get ready.

The first show was this afternoon.

Chet studied his face in the mirror set in one wall of the stateroom, picked up the dye kit, and sighed enviously as he thought of Jem's blond beard. All Kemrekl, as far as they knew, grew blond or reddish hair on their heads and faces. So Chet, with his close-cropped full beard of coal black, had the choice of depilating or dyeing. Since both he and Jem wore beards, Tina—xenologist and chief costuming consultant—had put the choice to both of them, with the stipulation that they both make the same decision. Both bearded and unbearded Kemrek cultures were known, but none in which members of either sex had individual option. The choice had been easy enough, but Jem had never stopped gloating over the fact that his natural beard color was close enough to skip the dye job.

Well, Chet thought as he set to work applying the dye, *at least we both have to put up with the wig bit.* That was because human and Kemrek scalp hair, in males, differed enough in structure so that a man's undisguised hair could attract dangerous attention. But a woman's . . .

He stole a sideways glance at Tina, seated beside him at the table that folded out of the wall. She had finished parting her hair in the middle, slightly heaped on top and falling over her shoulders in long, shiny waves, and was now applying bright red geometrical patterns to her forehead.

Chet didn't care for the face paint, but the rest of her costume he liked better than what was currently fashionable in the Capitol. It seemed vaguely unfair that she could look so good to him, as a human, and yet have to do so little work to pass for a Kemrek.

"You don't even have to put on a beard," he remarked suddenly.

She stopped what she was doing, looked at him, and giggled. "What?"

"You don't even have to wear a false beard. Or a wig. It isn't fair."

"Oh." She went back to her paint job, chuckling slightly. "Well, I can't help it if their women's hair is more humanlike than the men's. And there *are* cultures where the men wear beards and women don't. Why should I make extra work for myself?"

True enough, Chet conceded as he finished with the dye and tried on the wig, a shoulder-length mane of rather coarse and stringy blond fibers. Actually, he was quite impressed by the job Tina had done with the costume design, particularly on such short notice. The costumes, and in fact their whole assumed characters, were compounded from many known cultures, rather than trying to imitate any one. That way they could claim to be from a place no Kengmor had heard of, and not risk running into somebody who'd actually been there.

Chet completed his costume with a rather rakish purple cap. Then he stared at himself, suddenly stuck by just how good the make-up job was—and just how soon he was going to actually go out there among aliens and perform in it.

Tina noticed. "Stage fright?" she asked quietly.

He nodded. "Partly that, I guess. And something else. We thought it was pretty good that we could pass ourselves off as natives before, all wrapped up and very quiet and shy. Now in a few minutes we're going to go out in these getups and go around yelling, 'Hey, look at me!' Takes a bit of gall, doesn't it?" He laughed and stood up. "And of course, there is the fact that I haven't really done any magic to speak of for years. It's pretty rusty. Here, spray me." He handed her two small spray cans.

"You're in good company," she assured him, spraying the contents of one can uniformly over his coat and baggy pants. "I haven't done any acting since college." She finished the first can and repeated the process with the second.

"You make me feel much better," Chet grinned. "'Don't worry, it's my first operation, too.' Are we all set?"

"All set." Chet opened the door and let her precede him into the narrow corridor and forward to the main cabin.

Bydron Kel was already there, pacing nervously around near the hatch even though he wasn't going outside. When Tina stepped into the cabin, he almost swallowed his cigarette. "My goodness, Mrs. Barlin, are you going outside in *that?*" He stared wide-eyed at her outfit, consisting of light purple slacks with a metal chain-link belt and a matching sleeveless shirt with scarlet borders—long, loose-fitting, and open in front.

Chet could see her laughing inwardly, but to Kel she only said, as sweetly as possible, "Why, yes. Don't you approve?"

"I only—" he spluttered. "I mean, doesn't it increase the risk of discovery if they can see so—" He gave up, his face bright red.

"On the contrary," said Tina with the utmost dignity. "I should think that the less we have to hide, the less suspicion we should arouse." She stepped to the hatch and turned to wink at him. "And there *is* precedent, Agent Kel. I copied this design directly from a culture not two hundred miles southeast of here."

The Barlins stepped outside, the hatch swinging out to form a short ramp. The bowl-shaped field, largely covered with a low, dense, round-leaved plant, was more open than it had seemed from the air. The scattered trees had widely spreading tops, but beneath those canopies their yellow trunks occupied little ground. On the surrounding hills, however, thick tangles of vines made visitors unlikely.

Chet turned to look back at the boat. Out in the opening, its invisibility was much more striking. There was no visible trace of its presence except for the slight flattening of the ground cover under the hull and the open hatch that stood like a luminous-framed hologram in midair. Through the frame was the complete, three-dimensional, electric lighted world of a landing craft control room; around it, nothing but open woods.

Jem Wadkinz appeared in the picture frame, pushing the rustic but heavily ornamented wooden cart containing all the paraphernalia for their show. He appeared a little self-conscious in his wig and roomy magician's robe. Chet helped him ease the cart down the ramp to the ground. As soon as it was clear, Jem called back, "Okay!"

Stiv's voice answered from inside. "Good luck!" Then, with a faint whine, the ramp swung up and the boat vanished.

The effect was startling even to the initiated. "Weird," Tina said, looking around. "I feel even more isolated than I expected."

"Be sure to watch landmarks," Chet warned. He checked in his pocket to make sure the damping trigger was in place. Then they started off. He and Tina walked in front, side by side, while Jem alone pushed the heavy cart. They had both been apologetic about assigning him the slightly ignominious—and fatiguing—role of sorcerer's apprentice. But he didn't speak Lingmor, and Tina had been unable to find any precedent for treating him otherwise. Some conventions associated with traveling shows seemed much to well established to flout.

The hardest job of the day was the first: to find the least impossible place to go over the hill and through the barrier of vines. Once they got through and stood on the far side of the knoll, they had a good view of Yxyngar. The multitiered monastery, as in all such towns, dominated the landscape, but from here they could also see the periphery, the outlying region of tiny shacks with tall chimneys like English horns. And it was that, not the monastery, that was their destination.

Between here and there, the land was open and cultivated, broken by little except an occasional hut or spreading tree, and here and there a tiny moving figure or two. A narrow, slightly sinuous dirt road passed the bottom of their hill and took off across the fields for the town. Making sure no one was around, Chet helped Jem run the cart down the hill, but that was all the help he dared give. And Jem learned that the road was deeply rutted and pitted by dora hooves.

They trudged along, sniffing the slightly alien odors of recently cut plants and turned soil, until Chet saw a figure near the road a short distance ahead. He stopped. "Show time," he announced curtly. "Let us take a load off your hands, Jem." He reached into the cart, noticing that Jem was sweating rather freely, and pulled out two items. The flute—an ordinary bone flute, but with a very special, very unobvious attachment—he handed to Tina. The drum, with a cymbal and various other jingly things attached to it, he hung around his own neck.

And with a cymbal crash and a shout, he changed the whole mood of things.

"Onward!" he yelled in Lingmor. "Let's show them some magic!" And he beat out a fast, tantalizing cadence on his drum while Tina piped a wild tune and they marched along the road, Jem struggling to keep up.

The farmer looked up curiously as they approached. He was alone, stripped to a loincloth and broad-brimmed hat, pushing a wooden plow behind a huge dora. The animal's antlers were as imposing as on any Templeman's mount, but on the farms they were regarded more practically. On this one's left antler hung the farmer's shirt, and on the right a water jug and a pouch which probably carried his lunch. He paused in his work to watch their approach, and as they went by he grinned broadly and waved his hat at them. Then he went back to work, despite their waves and shouts of encouragement.

Chet saw disappointment in Jem's face. "There'll be others," he called back in Anglarneg, never slackening his noisemaking. "Just keep up the pace!"

They did, though they saw no more nearby farms for a

while. They passed a couple of roadside shrines—little birdhouselike affairs on posts, each sheltering an icon of the local dixar—and Tina called back to tell Jem what they were. At one point the road skirted the shore of an inlet, and at the closest point stood a rusty old cannon, aiming out over the water as if to defend the town. But a birdlike creature with vaguely reptilian head and tail was perched comfortably on the end of the barrel, leaning over to deliver a writhing worm to a gaping young beak sticking up from a nest in the muzzle.

Beyond the cannon, habitations began to appear. When they passed the first real house, they stepped up the racket. Chet barked extravagant claims of magical feats in Lingmor over the noise of the drum and flute, and Tina's gait became almost a dance.

And they picked up their first real customers. A peasant woman came out of a hut, with half a dozen offspring. Laughing and chattering too fast for Chet to follow, they ran and skipped along with the caravan. Two boys cheerfully gave Jem a hand pushing the cart. And as they passed other houses, more and more people of all ages—even a couple of farmers who did drop their work—joined the parade. They picked up quite a few when they dipped into the periphery and looped around a block of the dingy, smelly shacks. By the time they swung back to the road and headed back out of town, there must have been at least thirty—and a growing eagerness for the show to begin. "Now!" shrill young voices called out every time they came to a grassy spot with a shade tree. "Here!"

Of course, it would be poor showmanship to give in right away. But at the fifth tree out of town, Chet nodded to Tina and they led their piping and drumming to a shrill climax and motioned the cart off the road. The audience began squabbling for choice places in the shade. And Chet and Tina set to work helping Jem flip out the movable panels of the cart to convert it to a small stage.

They'd put a good deal of thought into that cart, and the conversion was quick. As soon as it was done, Jem sat in his assigned spot on it, quickly mopped his brow, and muttered, "That farmer had the right idea. We ought to get a dora!"

Then he became dutifully still. Tina struck a pose at the other rear corner of the stage. And Chet, moving with an air of growing mystery, sat cross-legged at stage front center, looking out over his eager audience and slowly raising his hands for silence.

He waited until he got it. And when he had had a full hush for a full half minute, he nodded slightly. Behind him, Tina raised the flute to her lips and her little finger flicked a concealed switch in the other end. An eerie tune began, winding slowly upward as Chet began to speak. (It was undeniably stage fright he felt, but he had performed enough to know better than to think about it. All that existed for now, was the audience and the show. . . .)

He had slipped the trigger into his palm and touched it once, and as he spoke solemnly of Mysteries from Afar, some of the audience began to nudge each other and point. It felt strange to sit rigidly, rising slowly two feet into the air, but it got their attention as few other things could have. They were not a cultivated audience, and before long their jabbers of excitement completely drowned his patter. When that happened he pressed the trigger again and began sinking back as the second layer of spraycoat vanished. The crowd became hushed again, and Tina's tune, which (with a little help from a computer) had been ascending steadily, now reversed and slid smoothly down the scale into subsonics. As soon as his feet touched the platform, Chet sprang upright, flinging his arms out in a flamboyant concluding gesture. The audience clapped and howled approval.

He had them! And he had the old, barely remembered feeling of what it was like to perform for an audience and have it work, and that gave him the confidence he needed to launch exuberantly into the rest of the show. The quasimaterial tricks were interspersed among conventional conjuring stunts, stunts he had done for friends at parties years ago and just recently begun dusting off again. He had feared they were too rusty. But they worked well enough and the feel was coming back. By the end of the show he found himself surprisingly caught up in the spirit of the thing and reveling in the applause. They raved about the finale—the quasimaterial ghost trick—and as they shouted and jumped Tina got out the box and began tossing tiny quasimaterial trinkets into the crowd. They scrambled to catch them; it was the custom for traveling troupes to distribute such samples at the end of the show, as an invitation to buy more. Several did, digging in the trinket box for things they liked and leaving hard little ceramic coins in exchange. They went away looking happy, and when they were sufficiently dispersed, Chet grabbed Tina and said gleefully, "They liked it!"

"Looks that way," she nodded. She smiled, but with restraint. "Looks that way, but let's not be too smug until we read the reviews."

Yes, Chet reminded himself sternly, silently, tempering his enthusiasm. *Time to remember it wasn't a show, first of all, but an experiment. But it* looked *all right. . . .*

They followed the road back to their hill at a much less frenzied pace, for Jem's sake if for no one else's. After they left the road, the landmarks they had noted guided them back to the boat.

They hoped.

With just a touch of doubt, Chet said loudly, "Open sesame!" To his relief—and not really very much to his surprise—a horizontal streak of luminous blue appeared several feet in the air and then yawned open into a door and a ramp. All three of them pushed the cart up inside. The hatch sealed itself behind them as Chet and Jem ran the cart aft to stow it. When they came back to the fore cabin, Tina was already in the corner consulting the PFSU—the psychocultural field survey unit. Jem disappeared without a word into the galley. Chet tossed off his wig and coat, stretched out in one of the passenger chairs, and lit up his pipe. Stiv and Kel were nowhere to be seen; Chet assumed they were napping in their staterooms.

He watched Tina consulting her pet oracle without much comprehension, but with some apprehension. Finally she turned away from it and looked at him with a broad, satisfied grin. "No problem," she announced. "Hardly a ripple, just like we told Doubting Tomas. And yes, Chet, they did like it! They thought it was a great show—and nothing more."

Chet relaxed into a grin as broad as hers. "Great!" he said with real relief. It could hardly have come out more perfectly—and so easily.

Jem came out of the galley just as Tina delivered her verdict. "Glad to hear it," he boomed, coming across the room with a pitcher of reconstituted beer and some glasses. "Let's celebrate." He poured glasses and offered them around; nobody refused. Then he lifted his own high, "A toast—to our scriptwriter. May she have a long successful run!"

Chet nodded and the two of them touched glasses. Tina beamed. Then they all enjoyed a well-earned, cold, refreshing drink.

Halfway through the first glass a strange, disconcerting thought flashed unbidden through Chet's brain. *Too perfect,* it said. *Too easy.* For a fleeting instant, he almost frowned.

Then he thrust the thought aside, held out his glass for a refill, and gave his whole attention to celebrating.

5

A dozen days after he first showed his work to Ravilyr, Terek knew the answer to Ravi's parting question. "What do the falling-body numbers have to do with it?" Ravi had wanted to know, and Terek had had to admit that he had only a nonrational suspicion that there was any connection at all. But now he knew. There had seemed to be a pattern in them, he had told Ravi then. This afternoon, as the thunder crashed around the monastery and the rain made dribbling and splatting noises on the pavement outside his study-chamber's window, he saw clearly what the pattern was. And it was so simple that he could state it in two or three brief sentences.

With no apparent exceptions—except for very special cases like dry leaves which were obviously affected by the wind as they fell.

Were there winds out in the heavens—out where the Wandering Stars wandered?

Terek didn't know. But suppose there weren't—or at least that the Wandering Stars, like a cannonball in a gentle breeze, were practically immune to their effects.

Then what?

He tried to think it out. The spoken language was awkward; he quickly resorted to the neater language of mathematics, in which his pattern looked even more trivial than in words.

He made several starts which led nowhere, crossed them out, and started over on fresh pages. Finally he was convinced that it was going to be no small job. He dimly sensed that someday, far in his future, somebody might bring a new kind of simplicity to this, too, but it was not at hand now. So he resigned himself to a long, tedious series of numerical calculations aided by sketches.

Consider a Wanderer, much less massive than the Day Star, here at a certain instant, and moving thusly. And now let go of it. Let it fall, if it will, toward the Day Star. Where will it be a bit later?

It didn't take long to see that it was falling with growing speed into the Day Star. He crossed it out and started over. *Suppose it's moving faster . . .*

Somewhere along there, the storm passed and the Day Star came out. The hour of the evening meal came and went without Terek's even noticing it.

Terek's second Wanderer spun off toward infinity—or toward the enormous black Starglobe which the Temple taught enclosed everything else. *I wonder,* Terek thought impishly as he scratched out that page, *if it will shatter when it hits. . . .*

Outside, the Day Star set. Gloom began to filter into the chamber. Terek paused only long enough to light a pair of candles.

By now he saw what he was looking for clearly enough to catch the next couple of unsuccessful tries before he had invested much time in them. And after just a few more, he made them converge on the one that worked.

He saw it working from the start. And, just as when he was working out the first circles with the Day Star at the center, he worked more and more feverishly as he saw it continuing to work. An hour after midnight, the circle he had been drawing piecemeal closed on itself and he stared at it, stunned by the beauty of it.

But he allowed himself only a few seconds to wallow in triumph. Then, with fierce determination, he started on another. This one at a different distance . . .

That one went faster. He was getting the hang of it now. He tried once more, this time daring to allow himself some careful approximations to speed the labor of calculation. But he finished it before the night was out, and by then the pattern was quite clear and quite familiar.

He got out the Ybhal papers and glanced at one thing in them—a thing he had previously noted on a scrap of paper under the heading "Periods."

A glance was all it took. Then he could contain himself no longer. Hastily gathering all the notes in his arms, he literally ran through the dark corridors, guided only by stray moonlight, and stood pounding on Ravilyr's door until it opened.

The night was not yet quite ready for dawn, and neither was Ravi. He appeared groggily, with a flickering candle in his hand and his robe thrown hastily around him. "What's all this?" he mumbled. "Terek? It's the middle of the night—"

"Not quite," Terek interrupted boisterously. "It's long past the middle of the night, and I haven't been to bed. But I've predicted everything about the Wandering Stars. Everything! Ravi—they're just falling bodies!"

Ravi blinked and then his eyes snapped wide open. Most of the confusion on his face gave way to a congratulatory smile. "That's . . . *excellent,* Terek! Come in, come in! You must show me right away." He turned and hurried back in to light more candles.

As Terek followed him into the dark room, he added, "And there's one more thing, Ravi. You remember I told you about the dream that started me on all this, the same morning the Ketaxil landed? Well, I understand it now. I not only understand the pattern in the numbers—I see how we can use it."

Finally, after reveling in Ravi's shared enthusiasm for over an hour, Terek gave in to fatigue and retired to his chamber to catch the sleep he had missed. He fell asleep at once, barely missing the dawn, and slept solidly until midafternoon. Then he got up, ate quickly, and hurried back to Ravilyr's door.

And found it closed and locked, with a strange Templeman standing beside it with a ceremonial lance as if waiting for someone. There was something odd in that. With a slight feeling of annoyance at the Templeman's presence, Terek reached out to knock on the door.

And the Templeman grabbed his wrist and held it firmly. "He's not in there," he said curtly. "What's your name?"

"Terek." He glared at the Templeman, wanting to tell him to let go of his arm, but not quite daring. "What's going on? I need to see my tutor."

"He's not here," the Templeman repeated. "Templeman Ravilyr is with the dixar. The dixar left word that you were to join them as soon as you arrived. Come along." He gave Terek's arm a rough tug.

"You can let go of my arm," Terek muttered. Surprisingly, the Templeman did.

Terek followed him through the elaborate maze of torchlit corridors and long winding staircases, climbing higher than he had ever been before. He had time to wonder what as going on—and to grow uneasy, for he had never seen the dixar before. The prospect was one that inevitably generated excitement—and a touch of fear.

They came at last to a short corridor with no more stairways opening off it—nor windows, branch corridors, or anything else except a single massive wooden door at the far end. A single Templeman, young, strong, and similarly armed with a ceremonial lance, guarded it, eyeing them curiously as they came to the top of the stairs.

Terek's escort stopped and turned. "Go and announce yourself," he said. "I'll wait here until you're inside."

Terek went forward, a trifle nervously and more than a trifle confused. But he let none of that show as he walked up to the guard and looked him squarely in the face. "I'm Terek," he said clearly. "I'm told the dixar Kangyr wishes to see me."

The Templeman nodded silently, like a statue, and turned to open the big door. He motioned Terek to precede him into the room, then flashed the dixar's salute across the room. "Disciple Terek, Your Holiness," he said. Then he turned and left, letting the door swing shut with a soft thud.

As Terek took in his new surroundings, he was both vaguely disappointed and shocked at the irreverence of his thoughts. The dixar looked just like a man—and a rather ordinary, shriveled, little, old one at that. His deep purple robe and his surroundings made a valiant effort to conceal that fact, but they lost out to his thin, wrinkled arms and face, the brittle finlike ridges on his head, his sunken mouth, and big yellowish eyes set way back under shaggy brows. He sat in a huge carved throne on a dais, at the end of a long polished table in which his reflection could be seen by flickering torchlight. The torches were distributed around the windowless room in sconces on all the walls. In the wall just above each torch, to take full advantage of its light, was a niche sheltering a highly stylized image of Kangyr—for the dixar was, as all connected with the Temple well knew, the literal incarnation of the Supreme Presence in this region.

At Kangyr's right side—but on the floor rather than on the dais, so his head was below Kangyr's—stood another Templeman, a big, slightly awkward-looking fellow named Xymrok. Terek knew him slightly, as Kangyr's closest associate and personal messenger boy, but only slightly. Symmetrically placed at the other side of the throne stood Ravilyr, his face showing an agitation for which Terek knew no reason.

And the dixar Kangyr was scowling, a strange, almost comical scowl compounded of what might have been anger and boredom. He was looking straight at Terek. Almost too late, Terek remembered the salute—the elaborate greeting he had been taught in childhood and then never before had occasion to use. He performed it selfconsciously; Kangyr waved the response in a way that seemed perfunctory. Then he spoke, in the voice of an old but far from senile man.

"So you're Terek," he said flatly. His eyes moved, looking Terek over, but otherwise his expression showed no change. "Your tutor—the Templeman Ravilyr—has told me of the work you have been doing in recent days." He paused. When Terek made no response, he added, "The work with the Ybhal manuscripts and the motions of the Wandering Stars. He showed me the . . . er . . . inscription which started you on this line of work."

He paused again, staring intently, apparently watching

for any little thing Terek might do. With growing discomfort, Terek tried to do nothing—except wait.

Finally Kangyr said, "Ravilyr tells me that, with this inspiration, you have succeeded in describing the paths of the Wandering Stars as circles centered on the Day Star. Is that correct?"

Terek nodded. "Yes, Your Holiness. Not *exactly* circles, you understand, but very close."

"I understand. The important point is that the Day Star is at the center, and Ymrek merely one of the circles, like one of the Wandering Stars. Is *that* correct?"

Terek stiffened, growing wary. "Yes, Your Holiness."

Kangyr nodded slightly. "Ravilyr further told me that you have most recently been able to summarize the behavior of both Wandering Stars and falling objects on Ymrek in a few very simple statements."

He looked at Terek expectantly. Finally Terek nodded. "That's right, Your Holiness."

Kangyr nodded more noticeably and then sat staring for quite a while. Then he leaned slightly forward and asked Terek earnestly, "Has it never occurred to you, my son, that the inscription which started you on all this was inspired by Opposed Powers?"

Terek was caught slightly off guard. He had half expected that Kangyr was leading up to something like this. But he had not anticipated—though he should have—that it would be phrased in such terms. He started trying to sweep mental cobwebs off his theology.

"Let me remind you," said Kangyr, "that there are powers opposed to the Harmony of the Supreme Presence. They work insidiously, Terek, but they work. You must be on your guard at all times. You are familiar with the Covenant from Before Time, of course?"

"Of course."

"And you understand it?"

"I believe so, Your Holiness."

"Good. I won't ask you to repeat it. But I will remind

you that it makes it very clear that whatever else may happen—and anything may—Ymrek will remain always at the center, a single solid point of constancy in the universe. Always. Surely you see the contradiction between that and your portrayal of Ymrek circling the Day Star. Don't you?"

"I admit that it seems so," Terek granted. "But—"

"But?" Kangyr echoed explosively, leaning sharply forward and slapping the tabletop with a disproportionately big gnarled hand. "How can you say *but?* How can you argue? The contradiction is unarguably clear and explicit." His tone mellowed slightly, but a sinister, threatening undertone still grated through it. "Surely you see that. You see, Terek, it's quite obvious that Opposed Powers have been responsible for leading you astray. Not your fault, of course. But we must not allow you to remain in their grasp."

Terek stared at him, his thoughts in turmoil. This was the *dixar*, he reminded himself. His Holiness. Not someone who should under any circumstances be thought of as pigheaded. And yet . . . "So what do you want me to do?" Terek asked tightly. "Give up my work?"

Kangyr nodded vigorously. "Yes. Exactly. Give it up. Recant. Repent. Return to the Truth." He pressed his lips tightly together and stared distantly at one of the wall icons of himself, waiting.

Terek fumed, simultaneously fearful and defiant. His stare crossed Kangyr's and came to rest on the emblazoned slogan on the wall over the dixar—the First Precept, written in the Old Tongue. *"Magnificent and infinitely varied . . ."* he read, and then he thought bitterly, *Well, not* quite *infinitely—*

The thought was blasphemy. He cut it off sharply and forced his voice to be calm. "But, Your Holiness, at least some of it cannot be given up. The observations of the Wandering Stars on which my work is based are ancient and well tested. They are the Truth which has long been fully accepted by the Temple and interpreted in terms of epicycles, with Ymrek at the center. I have used only the well-established numbers. All I have done is to provide a different way to look at them—"

"A way which is *wrong!* " Kangyr thundered.

"A way which is simpler," Terek corrected quietly. He looked directly at the dixar as he did so, with an unspoken plea for understanding. Why couldn't he make Kangyr see that there was neither malice nor danger in his work? "A way which is simpler," he repeated. "A way which contradicts none of the old observations—yet allows them to be described in terms of a few simple principles. I know Ravi has told you about my rules. Has he shown them to you?"

"Yes," Kangyr said disgustedly. *"Rules."* Icicles of contempt hung so heavily from the word that Terek was almost afraid to ask what Kangyr thought of them.

He said almost inaudibly, "And . . .?"

"I dislike them," Kangyr said flatly. And then he stopped.

It seemed a strange reaction. "Why?" Terek asked.

"I dislike them," Kangyr repeated, obviously annoyed by the question. "I have not yet finished putting my objections into words you can understand. But I know—I know beyond any doubt—that these rules of yours are wrong and dangerous thinking. The very notion of rules in such a case is wrong and dangerous thinking.

"You know it's wrong," Terek said, "and yet you can't tell me why?"

Ravilyr had been standing by so silently that Terek might almost have forgotten he was there. He still didn't speak, but the shock that registered on his face was strong enough to jolt Terek himself. Kangyr, on the other hand, let nothing show on his face beyond a slight upward jerk of his shaggy eyebrows. But his voice was very cold and haughty as he told Terek, "I need give no reasons intelligible to you, Disciple. I suggest you remember that you are addressing the Supreme Presence."

The reminder hit Terek like a slap. He hesitated before saying anything else, shocked first by the realization that he'd been talking as if he'd forgotten that—and then by the realization that he was thinking the offense over as if it warranted anything other than prompt and thorough repentance. But still he thought. He was not quite ready to fly directly in the face of Holiness. But he did find that he was struggling to decide just what he really believed, in an area where it was always assumed that there was only one possible answer.

Gently, Kangyr broke into his thoughts. His voice had softened amazingly. It seemed to Terek that the dixar was trying to be fatherly—and not succeeding as well as Ravi did without effort. "Recant, Terek," Kangyr was saying softly. "Let us show you how the Powers have led you astray. Let us lead you back."

Terek stared at the opposite wall, not knowing what to say or think. Confused, he let his eyes wander to Ravi's face as if seeking guidance. But Ravi, for the first time Terek could remember, seemed almost as lost as Terek.

Then, abruptly, his face brightened—just enough for his pupil of many years to recognize. "Perhaps, Terek," he said quietly, "you should tell the dixar what you told me this morning. About a use for your work."

Kangyr's eyes flicked sideways, as if he had started to glance sharply at Ravilyr and then thought better of it. Instead he focused with new intentness on Terek. "There's more?" he said. "Your tutor is quite right, of course. Please tell me about it."

Terek saw Ravi's idea and nodded. It seemed to him like a long shot. *But,* he thought suddenly, *maybe not quite as long as I would have thought an hour ago. . . .* "Gladly, Your Holiness," he said, drawing himself up. "But I must ask to tell it my own way. Let me begin with a question. How do our prospects look in regard to the Ketaxil?"

There was no doubt about it—Kangyr reacted strongly to the question. He didn't let it show for long, but for just an instant his forehead and eyes crushed themselves together in an intense frown. "I see no need to discuss that," he said.

"No?" said Terek, growing bolder. "Then how are we going to survive, Your Holiness? My question was rhetorical. Every Keldac knows how our prospects are—they're terrible. The Ketaxil are raiding the towns which used to be inland in ever-growing numbers. They're ruthless and they're strong and they have fast boats and deadly weapons like crossbows. And what do we have? A few dugouts and a few rusty cannons onshore, so big and cumbersome to handle that if one of them ever hits anything it's an accident. If we don't get something different, Your Holiness, they're going to wipe us out. They'll burn the crops and the periphery shacks, and when the periphery's gone, they'll burn the monastery. All the relics and writings, just like they did at Ybhal—"

"Be quiet!" Kangyr rasped. Terek stopped. Kangyr asked, "What does all this have to do with your work?"

"Simply this. If we learned to understand my rules well enough, at a practical level, we might be able to apply them to improving our defenses against the Ketaxil. For Yldac, and for all the other strongholds of the Temple."

The new mention of Terek's rules obviously annoyed Kangyr, but he could not conceal his interest in hearing more. "How?" he asked tonelessly.

"If we know the rules—and so far the Wandering Stars bear them out—maybe we can learn to do a better job of predicting where a cannonball is going to go. Maybe we can even learn to make it go where we want it to!"

Kangyr hesitated—barely perceptibly, but definitely. Then he said flatly, "A cannonball is not a planet. Repent, Terek! Of your own accord, or—"

And he was interrupted. For the second time in this whole meeting Ravilyr spoke—and this time it was more than a few mild words.

"Your Holiness," said Ravilyr, and Kangyr stopped and turned to stare at him. There was a tremor of fear in his voice, but he gulped and went on, "Your Holiness, forgive me, but I think Terek's work deserves more of a chance."

Kangyr was staring incredulously. "*What?*"

"I think there is enough merit in his defense suggestion," said Ravilyr, "and enough need for it, that it would be too hasty to make him stop at this point."

Kangyr looked as if he couldn't believe his ears. "Ravilyr," he managed to say finally, ominously, "are you defying me?"

"No, Your Holiness, but I love the Temple and do not wish to see it fall unnecessarily." Ravi's voice still shook. Terek had never seen his tutor afraid before—and he had never seen anybody proceed so steadfastly in the face of such obvious fear. He watched with renewed admiration as Ravi made himself say, "All I say, Your Holiness, is that if you force Terek to stop now, I will tell other Templemen what happened. And we will appeal to you in a body to reconsider."

Kangyr was stupefied, and suddenly Terek saw, with shocking clarity, why. His neglected understanding of Temple theology came to the fore and let him see the enormity of Ravi's offense. Factionalism in the Temple was unheard-of—especially such a thing as a faction directly opposing a dixar. That would practically make Ravi and all who joined him Opposed Powers—by definition.

And yet, even knowing that, Terek felt a surge of proud gratitude toward his tutor.

Kangyr, for now at least, did not see it quite as bluntly as Terek did. He stared at Ravi for a long time. "The Opposed Powers have you in their grasp, too," he said finally, choked. "We will *all* think this over at greater length before we say anything publicly about it." He turned to glare at Terek. "As for you, and your dangerous scribblings. I advise you as strongly as possible—the *Supreme Presence* advises you—to give it up. Now go. Both of you." He turned to the big Templeman who had been standing silently at his right and said darkly, "Xymrok, you will remain with me."

Terek waited for Ravi to reach him and they left together, with no more words spoken by anybody in the room. As Terek turned to go, he saw that Kangyr was again staring absently at one of the wall icons.

And as he glimpsed the unprecedented look on his tutor's face, he reflected that that last bit of advice came directly from the Supreme Presence. Yet the fact that Kangyr could be argued with indicated a certain ambivalence in the Temple's attitude on that point. . . .

As the door closed softly behind him and Ravi, Terek realized grimly that this was the first time in his life that any part of his mind would have dared consciously hold such a thought.

6

From somewhere off in the distance, a strange and yet somehow familiar sound drifted up to Terek's ears. He stopped writing and listened.

There was an insistent rhythmic thumping, and above that a fainter assortment of jingles, and possibly some sort of shrilly melodious piping. And voices—a general hubbub from a small knot of people, with occasionally some unintelligible shouts rising prominently above it.

It sounded, he thought suddenly, like an itinerant show coming into town in quest of an audience. And that started him thinking.

He strained his eyes, looking out toward the periphery in hopes of seeing what it was, but without success. The sound was coming closer, but the source remained hidden. Probably the players were already wending their way through the streets of the periphery, concealed among the shacks. They might or might not come in as far as Monastery Wall Street. But even if they did, he wouldn't be able to see them from up here on the second terrace. If he wanted to see them, he would have to go down to the streets and seek them out.

Did he dare? Could he spare the time?

Doubtfully, he looked back at the notebooks on his lap and piled on the warm stones around him. There was still much to do. His work had been progressing furiously for the last week or so, generating both satisfaction and a self-perpetuating urge to keep on.

And all the while rubbing against feelings of guilt and apprehension about the dixar Kangyr's opposition to it. A dixar's opposition was not be taken lightly—for the dixar was the Supreme Presence. And yet he still felt that the dixar did not understand, impossible though that sounded. A dixar not understand? It was a contradiction in terms!

And yet . . .

To add to the confusion, Ravi was not backing the dixar. He wasn't explicitly urging Terek on either, but Terek had a strange feeling that that was only because he knew it was unnecessary. He had left Terek to spend his time as he saw fit lately, with no assignments, and he was well aware that Terek had seen fit to spend it doing calculations on Wandering Stars and falling bodies. Lately, Ravi had even given him some encouragement by dropping not-very-subtle hints that the dixar showed signs of reconsidering and accepting Terek's work. Because its applications to defense were becoming very clear, and the need for improved defenses was becoming even clearer . . .

The jingles and shouts were growing louder. So was the temptation. Such work as Terek was doing became compulsive; he could easily become so absorbed in it that his thought processes saturated and became muddled. He was nearing that point now.

He really needed a rest. An outlander troupe would offer a welcome respite, and would only cost him a couple of hours. Besides, he thought with a chuckle, it's been too long since I saw one.

Almost convinced, but still hesitating slightly, he looked back at his open notebook. He really ought to finish what he was doing—

The drumming and piping and shouting became suddenly louder. Terek looked up, turning his head sharply to look for the source. And this time he saw it. He had a clear view down one dusty street, and the show people were crossing it. There were three of them, in colorful exotic robes and with a gaily painted pushcart—

And then they were gone, disappeared among the shacks again. He had only seen them for a few seconds, but that was enough to make up his mind. He slapped the notebook shut, gathered the whole pile, and hurried inside to leave them in his study-chamber. Then he was off, dashing through the corridors to an outer gate and then through the streets, following the sound.

He didn't notice the Templeman who left by the same gate two minutes later.

Troupes of outlanders giving shows and selling curios from afar were a common sight in the towns—though not as common now as before the Shakes—and Terek had never quite broken his childhood habit of joining the throngs that gathered around them. Magic was one of their main wares, and Terek liked to watch their transparent "tricks" and marvel at how easily the peasants and townspeople were taken in by them.

He learned quite early that this bunch was different.

He caught up with them at the edge of town, a thin cloud of dust swirling around the three outlanders and twenty or thirty shabbily clothed local men, women, and children. Already the occasion had become a party, the locals laughing and dancing as much as talking. The foreign music was strange, but its spirit infectious.

They stopped in a farmyard where a scattering of small trees gave a dappled approximation of shade. The outlanders began unloading boxes from their carts and folding out hinged wings from it to make a crude platform. The audience gathered in a semicircle, most of them sitting on the grass.

And Terek noticed with some surprise that the party included, at the rear, a burly, unfamiliar Templeman. That was strange. It was not common for those of the Temple to waste their time on itinerant magic shows, and Terek wondered if—

A sudden chill shot through him. This Templeman was not completely unfamiliar. Terek didn't know his name, or anything about him, but he had seen him around often enough lately to suspect that for some reason he was watching him.

Him. Terek.

Why?

Uncomfortably, Terek moved to the other side of the crowd, still eyeing the Templeman suspiciously while seeking a less conspicuous position. The Templeman stayed where he was, but he remained standing—and watching, it still seemed to Terek.

The show was ready to begin. The tall male foreigner sat cross-legged at the front of the stage and held his hands up for silence. Gradually, it came, and when it was complete, he began to speak while one of the others—the only woman and the smallest of the three—played a soft, very strange tune on a flute.

The seated man's patter was typical drivel about mysteries from a distant place. But his accent was one that Terek couldn't place, and that bothered him. Costumes meant nothing, of course; theatrical people wore garb that might bear no resemblance to what anybody normally wore at home. But Terek had trained his ear to the point where he could usually tell where performers came from by the way they spoke Lingmor. This one he didn't recognize at all.

And there was something else strange about this man—to put it mildly. As he sat, speaking quietly, he was rising gradually into the air.

Terek could see no means of support and no way a means of support could be concealed.

How were they doing it? It was very seldom that Terek saw a piece of "magic" he couldn't explain, and it annoyed him when he did. This one had him completely baffled.

Naturally the audience was impressed. The magician whipped them up to fever pitch, then sank back to the platform, leaped to his feet, and launched into a fast paced, entertaining show. There were plenty of the tricks that Terek saw through at once, but among them were also some of the frustrating, really impressive kind. Like the one where the woman held her head in a raging flame for a full minute and emerged unscathed. And the one where the apprentice showed the audience an empty bucket, the tall magician poured water into it, and then there was an engraved brick in the water. He reached into the water as if to pull out the brick, emerged empty-handed—

And the brick was gone.

Things like that bothered Terek—and won the crowd over completely. They had started out relaxed on the grass; as the show progressed, more and more of them stood up and edged closer to the stage.

And still the Templeman slunk around on the other side.

After a while, increasingly bothered by the tricks he couldn't explain and disconcerted by the Templeman, Terek turned as if to leave. He really ought to go back to work. . . .

Then he heard the tall male foreigner announcing, "And now, ladies and gentlemen, our grand finale." Terek stopped, hesitated, and turned back toward the hastily improvised platform.

"Before your very eyes, ladies and gentlemen," the outlander chanted, "this enchanted statue from a far corner of the world will vanish." The crowd pressed toward the platform for a closer look. Terek decided to stay it out and pressed forward with them, still careful to avoid the Templeman's direct view. Disappearing acts were popular, and he seriously doubted they could fool him on that one.

"On the count of three," the magician warned, "it will begin to vanish, and by ten it will be gone. One . . . "

Terek frowned. The statue, a foot high and gleaming metallically, was standing in plain view on the edge of the table. Weren't they going to cover it with a cloth?

" . . . two . . . "

Terek found himself staring with an intentness he had not known since his first magic show. Still the statue stood unprotected in the full light of the Day Star.

" . . . three . . . "

Was it imagination, or did the metallic luster being to dim?

" . . . four . . . five . . . "

By six there was no doubt. The once-solid statue had acquired a ghostly pallor. It form still shimmered unchanged, but was growing harder to make out against the background.

" . . . seven . . . eight . . . "

Now the background began to be visible through the statue.

" . . . nine . . . "

Only a mere suggestion, a faint, three-dimensional shadow, remained.

"Ten!" It was impossible to say exactly when the last remnant of shadow had passed away, but it was undeniably gone. The onlookers broke into ecstatic applause and even Terek shook with an excitement he had thought long outgrown. That was the most convincing bit of trickery he had ever seen, and he had to find out how it was done!

Muttering hasty apologies, forgetting his uneasiness about the Templeman, he began shoving toward the front of the crowd. On the platform, the performers, all smiles, acknowledged the applause. The woman reached into a box and pulled out a double handful of trinkets. Laughing gaily, she threw them out to the crowd.

And Terek stopped in his tracks, momentarily dumbfounded. It wasn't the sight of the woman's spread hands, which he suddenly realized had only five fingers apiece, but the behavior of the things she had thrown. They flew out over the crowd and fell, but they fell at widely different rates! One drifted slowly down near Terek; a small boy caught it and cried out at its impact. He dropped it—it fell slowly—and Terek picked it up. It felt strangely heavy. More trickery, he thought with a grin, recovering quickly from his surprise and moving forward again. Really first-rate . . .

Then he saw the Templeman looming in front of him and stopped again, and this time he did not recover. The Templeman threw a handful of the strange trinkets in his face, pointed, and roared with gloating laughter. Nearby heads turned toward Terek, and more and more peasants joined the Templeman's coarse mockery. Some began to throw things . . .

And Terek filled with something like horror as he realized what was happening. No! he thought in amazement, not heeding the rain of trinkets. I was so close! Can a few cheap tricks really kill an idea?

As the derisive hoots closed in around him, he felt for the first time a sinking fear that they could—and a defiant will to prevent it.

He never reached the platform.

7

During their first few days on tour, Tina had rapidly acquired a skill in finding the invisible boat which remained, at least to Chet, amazing. He always had to concentrate hard on landmarks, and sometimes stop and think twice about whether he was following the right ones. Tina didn't seem to have to think about it at all. Their return from Yldac was typical: she just pranced deftly through the shrubbery and at just the right moment sang out, "Open sesame!" By carefully following her steps, Chet and Jem managed to wind up safely inside the familiar cabin.

Chet always welcomed the return. The inside of the boat, being visible, felt a good deal more homey than the outside. As soon as he and Jem had stowed the cart aft and returned to the fore cabin, he tossed his Kemrek wig aside, stretched out in one of the padded flight chairs, and lit up his pipe. Then he noticed Stiv Sandor bending over the communicator with the panel off.

"Trouble?" Chet asked.

"Nah." Stiv reached into the open unit and popped the top off a transparent cylindrical chamber. "Routine overhaul. Have to refresh the vacuum in these things every now and then, and now seemed as good as any." He took a can of Instavac from a cabin under the console, emptied it into the vacuum chamber so it overflowed, and set the empty can aside. "How'd it go with you? Ready to move on?"

Chet shrugged. "Okay, I guess. Same as everywhere else, anyway." He noticed that Wadkinz had vanished into the galley for his customary post-show beer, while Tina had just as predictably gone straight to her beloved PFSU to read the reviews. The routine was getting a little tiresome. Chet was glad they only had to go through it a few more times before they could get down to their main job and then go home.

Stiv put the cap back on the vacuum chamber and pointed his damping trigger at it briefly. "You sound bored," he chuckled. "I thought you'd be a regular ham by now. Hopelessly hooked on show biz."

Chet grinned as he watched the quasimaterial liquid fade exponentially from the chamber, leaving an excellent vacuum and heating the surroundings only a few degrees in the process. "It gets to me once in a while," he confessed, "mainly at the end of a show. They really go for that ghost trick." *Which*, he reflected, *amounts to nothing more than what you just did.* "But it's the same everywhere. They're impressed and intrigued, but not unduly. They've seen so little of the planet for themselves that nothing we claim to bring from another part of it really surprises them. We haven't seen any evidence yet that there's going to be any problem getting them to take a few quasimaterials in stride, and I couldn't see anything different here." He looked across the room. "Could you, Tina?"

Tina, uncharacteristically, was frowning. "Not out there," she said cryptically. "But, Chet, come here and take a look at this."

"Better go," Stiv said, turning back to the communicator. "She sounds worried."

She does indeed, Chet thought as he went to join her. *Now, why should that be?*

The psychocultural field survey unit was one of the main tools of the modern anthropologist, psychologist, or xenologist. It would provide, quickly and more or less measurably, information which could be only crudely and laboriously approximated by any other method. But its use required a formidable complex of highly refined, subtle skills—akin to those demanded by the polygraph of centuries earlier, but orders of magnitude more difficult. Tina, educated and employed as a xenologist, had those skills. Chet, whose work as a comparative historian brought him into contact with dead cultures more often than living ones, didn't—or, more precisely, he had them only in the most rudimentary form. Consequently, his look at the crowded panel of meters, color bars, and chart recorders failed to tell him what had Tina so upset. He wound up staring blankly and asking, "Well, what's it say?"

"This place *isn't* like the others," she explained. "It seemed like it, out there, just watching the audience. But there's a lot we didn't see, and I'm not sure what it is. Look here." She pointed at some multicolored wiggles and spikes on a roll chart. "This is the time of our show. I can't correlate it down to the minute, but it's in this neighborhood. All through it there's a pattern of unusual activity, highly localized and increasingly intense. I've never seen anything quite like it before, but I'd say it looks like a single highly intelligent mind in a state of great agitation. Look at this shock here."

Chet looked, but it didn't mean much to him. "Can you tell any more?"

"General location—right around that farmyard where we gave our show. It could have been somebody in the audience."

Chet nodded, then brightened. "That little brawl we saw starting up in the audience after the show . . . could it have something to do with that?"

Tina shrugged. "I don't know. I didn't pay much attention at the time. It just looked like typical peasant rowdiness. Didn't seem to have much to do with us."

"That's what I thought, too. But now that I think back . . . Tina, did you notice that there was a Templeman in that brawl?"

"Hm-m-m. Yes, now that you mention it. Was he actually brawling?"

"I'm not sure. Did you catch anything they said?"

"Afraid not. I was kind of busy, there were too many of them talking at once, and they were talking too fast for me. My Lingmor isn't *that* good."

"Neither is mine. And Jem's is practically nonexistent. But I don't remember ever seeing a Templeman at one of our shows at all, before this. The more I think about it, the more I suspect . . . I don't know what." Unable to pursue the line of thought, Chet bit his lip and looked back at the PFSU traces. Now that they were pointed out to him he could recognize the highly abnormal character of those patterns. And he could see, faintly, some of the possible implications. But he couldn't follow the interpretation into the present. He waved a hand toward the group of readings they had been discussing and asked. "Then what?"

Tina motioned at some later charts, and then at screens showing live displays of current monitorings. "It continues. There are a couple more distinct jolts. Then a few other patterns become prominent, too. The locale changes—it seems to be in the monastery now. Rather far into the monastery, in fact—possibly even in the castle itself. But all the unusual activity remains clustered around the one we saw first."

Even with Tina's guidance, Chet could follow only the barest outlines through the PFSU's maze of output. But he thoroughly trusted her interpretation, and it wasn't hard to see what the pattern she was describing might mean. "Some bright boy's onto us?"

Tina nodded. "That's my guess. Somebody who came to our show and recognized that we're not just another band of gypsies from over the hill. He has suspicions about us—powerful suspicions, and a powerful determination to do something about them." She waved a hand at the real-time displays. "Now this. Does this mean that not only does he suspect, but he's already gone straight to the local priest-king and got *him* scared of us?"

"It could," Chet said grimly. "Of course, it could mean something else, too. You still haven't taught that thing to read actual thought content, have you?"

"Not a chance. That's what's so maddening. All we can see are prevalent attitudes, emotions, mental tones. But when we see a pattern like this we can't resist guessing what's behind it. Our guesses may be all wet, but we worry about them anyway."

"True." Chet couldn't deny that he was worried by these. "It fits together too well, Tina. I don't like it."

"Neither do I. Where do we go from here, Chet?"

"Yjhavet's next on the list," Chet said unnecessarily, "but I see what you mean. I think it's conference time." He looked wistfully back at the PFSU readouts and added, "Too bad, too. After Yjhavet there were only supposed to be two more. Routine and easy."

Kel chain-smoked. He sat in the pilot's throne, swiveled around to face the curved row of passenger seats, and listened with plainly visible discomfort as Chet and Tina told him of the new development. He puffed incessantly and nervously on long thin cigarette after long thin cigarette, and the parts of him that weren't busy smoking found other ways of fidget. He sat impatiently through Tina's exposition of what the PFSU had told her. When she finished, he cleared his throat and complained, "Really, Mrs. Barlin, I hardly see that there's any great problem. If there's a chance we've been discovered here, we move on to the next place without further ado. It's as simple as that. The bulk of the data was typical, wasn't it?"

"Yes," Tina granted, "but you underestimate the possible importance of a sufficiently atypical individual—not to mention the Temple of the Supreme Presence. In case you've been neglecting your brief, let me remind you that the Temple is behind this whole renaissance we're supposed to be protecting. Do you know what the dixarl are, Agent Kel?"

"Of course I do," Kel said indignantly. "The priest-kings."

"Not bad, for a near-translation. Chet and I've used the term ourselves on occasion, even though we realize it's only a rough approximation. Suppose that's all there is to it, for the moment. Priest-kings. The whole culture is a theocracy: church and state are inextricably entwined. A dixar directly controls every town in Yngmor. We're afraid somebody has told the one in Yldac about us, and he's getting edgy."

"So we leave," Kel retorted tiredly. "Fast. Without a trace. So he never gets a chance to check up on his suspicions, and in a few days he forgets about us."

"It's not that simple," said Chet. "They communicate. Suppose he tells his counterparts in other towns to keep an eye out for us."

"I thought they *didn't* communicate, because they can't. That's why we're here, remember?"

"That's *almost* why we're here," Chet corrected. "They don't communicate as well as they need to, but a message gets through now and then. One might be all it takes."

"And even if that doesn't happen," Tina added, "think of what can happen right here in Yldac. Suppose whoever tells the dixar here about us is somebody he really trusts. So even if we get out without leaving a single trace he can check up on personally, he assumes his informant was telling the truth. He assumes we're real and we simply slipped away—which is exactly right. But maybe he suspects we'll be back, and he draws his own interpretations of who we were and what we were up to. Maybe he thinks we're dangerous—so he starts warning his subjects about us. They develop their own prejudices about us. Then, eventually, somebody does make it to another town—"

"This is silly," Kel interrupted. "Who's going to believe him? Some of *them* have seen us with their own eyes, and they know *he* hasn't. He's just a distant old man who lives alone up in the castle where nobody ever sees him, and makes decrees. He's something they endure because they have to, that's all. They don't have to *listen* to him."

Chet and Tina stared at him silently for several seconds, honestly amazed at the depth of his misconceptions. Finally Chet said, "You don't understand *anything* about this, do you? You're trying to understand it in terms of human history—and even your conception of that is a little blurry. Don't you realize what else the dixarl are?"

"I can see you're going to tell me whether I say I do or not," said Kel, "so don't let me stop you." Affecting indifference, he lit a new cigarette.

"They are," Chet explained slowly and carefully, "the Supreme Presence."

Kel's indifference shaped itself abruptly into a puzzled

frown. “What are you talking about, Barlin? I thought the Supreme Presence was their god.”

“That’s about as good a translation as ’priest-king’ is for ’dixar,’” said Tina. “At best. Actually, their concept of the Supreme Presence seems to be rather different from any human idea of a god, though it has a little in common with some forms of pantheism. We still don’t have a completely clear picture of it. In fact, there’s a good deal we don’t really understand about the whole Temple philosophy. The Templemen themselves don’t claim to be able to tell you exactly what the Supreme Presence is. Their scholars spend their whole lives striving to develop an intuitive understanding of its True Nature.”

“But we do know,” said Chet, “that the dixarl are considered literal embodiments or foci of it. If you offend a dixar, you offend the Supreme Presence itself. If a dixar tells you something, that’s a direct revelation of the nature of the universe. The possibility that he’s lying or mistaken is literally unthinkable. There isn’t even any direct or grammatically correct way to say it in their language.”

“So you see,” Tina finished, “if we get *them* down on us, the project has unequivocally had it. Very probably, so have we.”

Kel said nothing. He seemed to ignore her sarcasm, and the face he made seemed to say merely, *Why does life have to be so complicated?*

“Look at it this way,” Chet suggested. “If there’s a chance we’ve been discovered, it’s especially important that we stay here long enough to make sure. If it *has* happened, we have to know about it and see if we can undo any damage the discovery’s caused.”

“Exactly what,” Kel asked slowly, “are you asking permission to do?”

“Investigate,” said Chet. “Go into town and poke around—cautiously, of course—to find out exactly what’s happened. And if we have been found out, we’ll have to take appropriate action.”

“Meaning?”

“For starters, no Project Airfloat—and who knows what

else? Whatever it takes to minimize whatever impact we've had beyond what we intended."

"This poking around in town," Kel pointed out, "involves risks far beyond what we'd calculated. Suppose we *haven't* been discovered yet. You might be found out in the act of trying to verify that we haven't. Kind of self-defeating, isn't it?"

"We'll have to be very careful." Chet looked straight at Kel. "But we have to know. This started out to be very small, very cautious intervention justified by special circumstances. They're not special enough to justify any more than that, Agent Kel. You know that . . . don't you?"

Slowly, as if suddenly painfully aware that he didn't really want this responsibility, Kel nodded.

8

Terek didn't struggle, of course. He did experience a brief impulse urging him to do so, but as the first half-dozen hands clamped themselves roughly upon him, he realized quickly that any attempt at resistance would be utterly futile—and might hurt him indirectly later on. So he stood steadfastly—inwardly seething, outwardly enduring with dignity—as the peasants pressed in around him. Their hands tore his clothes and scratched and bruised his body; their inarticulate derision echoed shrilly in his ears.

And none of them, he found time to observe with bitter irony, *know what they're doing. They're a mob, pure and simple.* The Templeman made short, agitated little dashes back and forth around the gathering knot of tormentors, egging them on with a strident tirade against the stupidity of Terek's theories, almost shrieking to make himself heard above their racket. They knew nothing of Terek's theories and cared less; what the Templeman said was so much babbling. But he was a Templeman and he was clearly urging them to grab this stranger and taunt him for *something* he had said. That was all they needed.

The outlanders, joking among themselves as they packed the trappings of their show back into their cart and prepared to move off, cast casually curious glances this way and then went about their business. Meanwhile, the random fistfalls and taunts gradually focused themselves on a goal. "Hold him!" the Templeman yelled. "Don't let him run. We must take him at once to the monastery. Drag him along—for the dixar Kangyr!"

They dragged him, all right. It was quite unnecessary,

of course. He would have walked exactly where they wanted, with no attempt at resistance, if they had let him. What else could he do? But they would have none of it. The primitive instincts were aroused and were not to be subdued. The Templeman himself had commanded them to drag him, for the dixar. So drag him they would, striving mightily to outdo each other, each hoping to impress the Templeman with his zeal in serving the Supreme Presence.

So he bounced along the road, jerked this way and that, choking on dust kicked in his face, thoughts drowned in cacophony. He had no real chance to reflect on the significance of what was happening to him as they followed the narrow lane back to the edge of town and through the periphery (attracting several more curiosity seekers) to Monastery Wall Street.

There the Templeman worked his way around to the front of the crowd and barked orders to stop in front of a huge wooden door in the high stone wall. He pushed roughly through the peasants, grabbed Terek by the arm, and hauled him to the front of the crowd. He stood there, holding Terek firmly with one beefy paw while the other lifted a huge knocker in the form of an icon of Kangyr and let it fall three times. He waited for several seconds, the magic-show crowd chattering excitedly among themselves, then repeated the knock. This time the door opened almost instantly, slowly and squeakily. Another Templeman stepped forward out of the gloom, leaning on a ceremonial lance and peering at the visitors with eyes not yet adjusted to bright afternoon light.

"I must take this Disciple to the dixar Kangyr," Terek's captor muttered to the door guard. Then he turned to the crowd and shouted, "You have done your duty. Now go home!" And without waiting for a reply, he turned back to the door and shoved Terek through. As the door swung shut behind them, Terek heard the jabbering outside fade to a disappointed almost-silence as the deflated crowd dispersed. The door shut off the last of that, and in the sudden gloom and stillness, the realization could finally reach him.

And the fear.

Heresy would be the charge, he knew, or something very much like it. Such a thing was rare—almost unheard-of. But once when he was very small, he had seen an execution. There was a special walled-off courtyard in an obscure corner of the monastery, with tiered platforms for spectators to stand around the firepit under the gallows. Terek remembered being utterly bewildered as he watched the unknown adult squirming on the end of the rope. Trying futilely to cry out as he was lowered slowly into the flames. . . .

It was not a pretty picture. He could verbally imagine, but not really grasp, the imminent likelihood of his own being the next man on the noose.

Oddly, as they wound higher and higher along the twisting corridors and stairs, the personal impact of the danger was not even foremost in his mind. He found himself thinking far more of two remoter consequences. The first concerned Dajhek and Tolimra. When he had first become a Disciple, Ravi and his colleagues had wanted him to live at the monastery, as most Disciples did. He had refused to leave home (and Dajhek and Tolimra had backed him up)—originally for typical childish reasons backed by more than typical childish stubbornness, years later because of the blunt realization that if he didn't care for them in their old age, no one would. Now if he was executed, his care would end, and they would not long outlast it.

The second thing haunted him was the thought of his work dying with him. He was sure now that he could use his laws to predict. And he sensed more powerfully every day that the whole project had an importance far larger than he had yet been able to see clearly.

They came to the highest corridor, the short one with no outlet but the stairway at one end and the big guarded door at the other, which Terek had seen only once before in his life. His escort loosened his grip on Terek's arm, as if any attempt at resistance or escape was inconceivable in this place.

The guard at the door was the same one Terek had seen

there before. He had been leaning a bit too casually on his lance and stiffened abruptly at their approach.

"The dixar will wish to see me immediately," Terek's captor informed him curtly. "The Disciple will go in with me."

The guard nodded and ushered them in, much as he had ushered Terek in alone before. But this time Terek was closely and attentively followed, and the dixar Kangyr sat alone at the end of his table.

Kangyr looked up with obvious interest—and perhaps a touch of strangely colored pleasure—as the guard silently saluted him and went out. Terek also gave the salute, but his heart was hardly in it. Kangyr flashed the response, and then a cryptic half smile crept over his features. When he spoke, it was not to Terek, but to the big Templeman who had brought him. "Ah, Jhalat, I see you've brought me company. You have news, also?"

Jhalat had let go of Terek altogether. He moved closer to the dixar. "Yes, Your Holiness. I believe I've found the way to silence Terek's misthoughts once and for all."

Kangyr showed no expression beyond the faintest possible suggestion of a nod. "Tell me about it," he said.

"Very well, Your Holiness." Jhalat adjusted his posture, standing very erect and looking not quite directly at the dixar's face. "As Your Holiness requested, I've been watching Disciple Terek for several days, watching for just such an opportunity. Today I followed him to a roving outlanders' show."

"Odd," Kangyr observed. "What prompted you to go to one of those, Terek?"

"I needed a rest." Terek said. "I often used to go to the shows, when I was younger. I like to see how their magic was done. So when I heard one today, I went."

"It will be interesting," said Jhalat, "to see how he explains some of this magic. There were several rather amusing demonstrations in the outlander's show, Your Holiness—not that I approve of such pastimes, you understand. At the end of the show the performers, as usual, distributed samples of their wares. Among them were these." He reached into his robes and pulled out a handful of trinkets. He laid them all on the table and then selected two from among them, a pair of white spheres a couple of centimeters in diameter and apparently identical in all respects except that one of them had a thin, wavy red line around its equator. "Watch closely, Your Holiness." He held the plain ball out and let go of it. It seemed to hesitate and then, slowly—unnaturally slowly—fell toward the floor. A full second or more later it was only halfway down.

While it was still in the air, Jhalat released the red-lined ball from the same spot. It plummeted almost too fast for the eye to follow, overtook the first ball, deflected it slightly as it hit and bounced off, and reached the floor first. It bounced and rolled off toward a corner while Jhalat bent down to scoop up the slow ball. "As I recall," he said as he stood back up, "Terek has told us that all objects should fall at the same speed." He waited expectantly.

Kangyr nodded slightly and turned solemnly to Terek. "Well, Terek, what do you have to say about this? Are you ready to renounce your folly?"

"No, Your Holiness," Terek said quietly. Kangyr's eyebrows shot up. "It is not folly . . . Your Holiness."

"How," Kangyr grated, gesturing angrily at Jhalat's pile of souvenirs, "do you account for what we just saw?"

"And the others," Jhalat added. "There were other demonstrations, Your Holiness, that clash just as violently with Terek's so-called rules. Shall I show you—"

"No need." Kangyr waved the suggestion aside. "I have seen this one and I have your word for the others. Answer me, Terek. How do you reconcile these events with your ideas?"

"They're tricks," Terek said stubbornly.

"Tricks? Then tell me, Disciple. How are these tricks done?"

"I don't know. But they're tricks nonetheless." Even as he talked, Terek wondered at his own arrogance, standing here on the brink of a death sentence, flatly contradicting His Holiness. Yet he couldn't quietly accept the accusations, do what Kangyr wanted, and let his work fade away. Part of him shook and urged him to take the easy way out, to be sure his own skin was safe, but another part shouted that he must resist as long as any resistance was possible. With visions of the execution pit flaming in his head, he said, "Please, Your Holiness. The fact that I can't explain these tricks doesn't change the fact that I do understand Wandering Stars and cannonballs. Can't—" He stopped abruptly, suddenly wary of going too far.

"Can't what?" Kangyr prompted stonily, when he had waited several seconds for Terek to finish.

"Nothing, Your Holiness," Terek said almost inaudibly, staring down at the tabletop.

There was a long silence. Finally Kangyr said quietly, "I think Ravilyr should be present for the rest of these proceedings. Jhalat, would you go and have him summoned? Terek, you wait where you are."

Jhalat went out. The door thudded gently shut behind him. Kangyr said nothing. He didn't even look at Terek, but simply sat staring with much the same scowl Terek had seen on his face at their first meeting. Terek stood watching him silently, trying to understand. Minutes passed; how many, Terek could not say because he was too agitated to trust his subjective time sense. But he had plenty of time to turn his situation over in his mind—and to grow steadily more apprehensive about its outcome. The one ray of hope he could see was that Ravi would be here for whatever else happened. Surely he would come to his pupil's defense.

Although, now that Terek thought about it, it was not at all clear just how much good that would do. After what had happened the last time the two of them faced Kangyr . . .

Finally the door opened again. Terek heard two pairs of footsteps behind him, and Kangyr waved a return salute. The footsteps separated and a brown-robed Templeman strode toward Kangyr along each side of the table, Jhalat on Terek's left and Ravi on his right. Jhalat went quite close to Kangyr; Ravi stopped halfway and turned so he could see both his dixar and his Disciple. The concern on his face was obvious, but he said nothing. He looked for several seconds at Terek, then turned expectantly to Kangyr.

Kangyr nodded slightly toward him. "How much has Jhalat told you of why I've called you here?"

"Only that Terek was in trouble, Your Holiness," said Ravi, his voice low and expressionless. "And that I must come at once."

Kangyr nodded again, with a wry suggestion of a smile. "A fair enough statement. Terek is indeed in trouble. You see the pile of objects there on the table?" He gestured slightly.

"Yes, Your Holiness."

"Do you know what they are?"

"No, Your Holiness."

"They are trinkets distributed by a troupe of outlanders after a magic show near here. Jhalat brought them back because they have some rather interesting properties. Terek saw their show, so he is well aware of those properties. Terek, pick up the white ball."

Terek did so without looking at Kangyr or making any verbal acknowledgement.

"Ravilyr, please watch this carefully. Terek, drop the ball onto the table."

Terek looked at Kangyr and then to Ravilyr. Then he let go of the ball. Ravi's eyebrows rose as it fell. Terek caught it to keep it from rolling off the table, returned it to the pile, and stood waiting, watching Ravi's face anxiously.

"I think," said Kangyr, "there is little need to add anything to that demonstration. I think it is quite obvious that this ball does not behave according to Terek's so-called rules. Can you deny that?"

"No, Your Holiness. But . . . may I see the ball, please?"

Kangyr hesitated briefly, then nodded to Jhalat. Jhalat walked to Terek's end of the table, picked up the ball, and handed it to Ravi. Ravi examined it closely, hefted it, examined it again, and dropped it twice. A puzzled frown slowly grew on his face. He took a coin from his robe and dropped that. Finally he took his coin in one hand, the outlanders' ball in the other, held them both as high above the table as he could, and dropped them both at the same time. There was no possible doubt that the coin fell much faster.

He put the coin back in his robe and handed the ball back to Jhalat. "Thank you, Your Holiness," he said quietly, not looking at the dixar.

"So you are quite convinced," Kangyr said with satisfaction. "The ball does not obey Terek's whims. Neither do several other objects in the outlanders' show. The conclusion is quite plain."

"Where are these outlanders from?" Ravi asked suddenly.

"How could that possibly matter?" Kangyr looked away, concentrating absently on one of the wall icons. "The point is simply that they have artifacts which do not follow Terek's rules—and therefore demonstrate quite unarguably that his rules are not rules at all. And, that having been done, any further consideration of them is out of the question."

"But, Your Holiness," Ravi said with obvious surprise which Terek didn't completely understand. "I thought—"

"Terek," Kangyr interrupted, ignoring him, "still seems to have difficulty understanding this. So I hoped that as his tutor you could help. Perhaps we can avoid the need for any unpleasant measures." The way he said it was distinctly unpleasant.

Ravi turned to Terek. "What do *you* say, Terek? Do you deny that the tricks violate your rules?"

"I don't deny that they *appear* to," said Terek. "Any fool can see that. I do deny that they disprove my rules. I don't know why they act the way they do, but I do know that some things do obey my rules. Maybe even these do and there's just some trick to create the illusion that they don't. Or maybe my rules apply only to certain kinds of objects and these are a different kind. I don't know."

Ravi kept looking at him, as if waiting for more. When none came, he turned back to Kangyr. "I have nothing to add, Your Holiness," he said quietly. "Though the ball I saw did seem to be a kind of material I've never seen before . . ."

Kangyr's eyebrows jerked upward. "Are you defending him?" he demanded incredulously. He leaned forward, hands pressed hard against the tabletop, jaw thrust forward, glaring piercingly, accusingly, at Ravi. "Answer me, Ravilyr. In the face of what you've seen here, are you defending Terek's heresy?"

Terek tensed. Hardly breathing, he watched, waiting for his tutor's response. Ravi stared fixedly at Kangyr for a long time, his face rigid and hard to read. When he finally spoke, his voice was low and shook slightly. It was obvious to Terek that there was more fear than he liked to admit among his motivations. He said quietly, "No, Your Holiness. My feelings on this subject are well known. I have nothing to add." He turned to Terek. "The only advice I can give to you, Terek, is to be true to yourself. For ultimately no man can act except on the truth as he himself sees it." Then he turned quickly away, as if he could no longer face Terek, and stared blankly at the tabletop.

Terek was stunned by the triteness and apparent cowardice of Ravi's reaction. But he bore Ravi no real malice; even then he could sympathize with his tutor's position. Ravi's last words even nerved him to take what he knew might be his last chance to repeat his explicit warning. He stood straight and looked defiantly at Kangyr. "Ravi is right, Your Holiness. I've told you the truth as I see it, and I've seen no reason to change it."

"*I* have told you you must change it," Kangyr growled.

"But you haven't shown me any reason to doubt my work."

Abruptly, Kangyr reached out and snatched the slow-falling ball from Jhalat. He hurled it at Terek's chest; it flew fast and very straight, thrown hard enough to hurt when it hit. "I've shown you nothing? Kangyr demanded. "You call this nothing?"

"I've already told you," Terek answered quietly, boiling inside. "There's no point in repeating it. I don't know what that ball is or where it came from or how it works. But none of that matters. It has nothing to do with my theories. Make a cannonball or a cobblestone fall like that and maybe I'll have to reconsider. But not this."

"A cannonball or a cobblestone *could*," Kangyr assured him. "'Magnificent and infinitely varied—'"

"I know all that, Your Holiness," Terek interrupted. "You tell me they *could* fall like that, but in my experience they *don't*. Can you show me one that does, Your Holiness?"

All three Templemen's mouths dropped wide open. Kangyr stammered, "I—"

"I would think," Terek drove on recklessly, "that if you really want me to believe that, it would be no great task for you to show me. I mean, you being the incar—"

"Terek!" Ravi interrupted sharply, looking up with shock strong on his face. "Terek, don't be crazy."

Kangyr had recovered enough of his composure to say very deliberately, "Why should I care what you believe, Disciple?"

"I don't know," Terek said. "I honestly don't know." He had caught the warning in Ravi's voice; he was well aware that he was already far beyond the limits of good judgment. And yet he went on, getting in deeper and deeper. He finished, "But it's pretty obvious that you do care. You don't look exactly indifferent."

Kangyr pressed his lips tightly together, fixed his gaze on an icon, and fumed silently for half a minute. Terek said quietly but with determination, "Whether you care what I believe or not, Your Holiness, you need to be interested in my ideas. You need my rules." He saw Kangyr about to interrupt and just went on, a little faster and with even more determination. "No, wait. Please listen. The first time I met you we talked about this. That was just a few days ago. Then I said we needed my rules because the Ketaxil are a threat to our civilization that we can't hope to hold off with our present defenses and the rules might improve our position by letting us aim our weapons more reliably. All I said about the Ketaxil threat, then, was what we already knew about it. All I said about the validity of my rules was that so far the Wandering Stars bore them out and maybe we could learn to apply them. Well, Your Holiness, you know as well as I that there've been rumors ever since the Ybhal relics were rescued that the Ketaxil are developing ever deadlier methods of attack. Their raid a few weeks ago made that at least believable—they'd never managed to actually land men here before. In these last few days I've heard new rumors that they're planning a return with new types of weapons. You've probably heard them, too. Can you afford to ignore them, Your Holiness?

"Meanwhile, in these same days I've done more work with my rules. *I can use them*, Your Holiness, *now!* I have them worked down to the practical level where I can use them to predict. And I've tested some of the predictions not just with Wandering Stars but with small everyday objects right here in Ymrek. Things like we'll have to use to defend ourselves—"

"Enough!" Kangyr exploded, furious and incredulous. Terek stopped and stared, breathing hard, as Kangyr spat out, "It's incredible that anyone can persist in such folly even in the face of such direct evidence. Even in the face of the explicit word of a Holy Dixar that it's folly!" He shook his head, staring wildly, then stopped abruptly, staring as if his gaze should nail Terek to the wall. His voice turned suddenly deadly serious. "Obviously words alone will not put an end to it."

Terek felt an instantaneous jolt of wild fear—

—which dissolved into a mixture of relief and disgust as Kangyr finished. "There's no possible way to regard you except as a Dunce." Then, peremptorily, "Get him out of here. Jhalat, see that the appropriate things are done. Ravilyr, you may stay here. I'd like a few words with you." He sat back and dismissed the others with a shrug and a wave.

And again Terek was being dragged. With obvious relish, Jhalat dug powerful fingers into his arm and off they went, while Ravi looked after with a deeply pained expression. Out through the door, past the guard in the corridor outside, and down stairway after stairway, Terek bouncing roughly and struggling to keep from stumbling. At first they retraced their path up to the dixar's chambers, but on the third level they left it and Jhalat hauled him through a narrow, dark, smelly, low-ceilinged corridor with rows of small plain doors along both sides. Jhalat pounded the doors with his free hand as they passed and bellowed, “To the wall! To the wall! We have a Dunce!” His knocks and shouts echoed back and forth off the hard stone walls, ringing the length and breadth of the corridor.

At the end was a larger door with relief carvings and polished metal ornaments. Jhalat threw it open just enough to show what it was; the refectory, a cheerily lighted hall rising two full levels to its ceiling, crisscrossed with massive wood beams. Fifteen or twenty robed Templemen sat around the tables, eating, drinking, talking. Jhalat stuck his head in and shouted over their noise, “A Dunce, Templemen, a Dunce! Bring the vestments!”

Without waiting for reply, he gave Terek’s arm a hard jerk and they were off again, retracing their steps along the corridor. Behind them, in the big hall, the dining table chatter faded very briefly to a startled pause, then exploded into a boisterous roar that kept growing and spilled out the door to follow them down the hall. Already Templemen were streaming this way; here and there chamber doors flew open along the corridor and others popped out to join them.

Two more levels and they stepped out into the fresher air of the cobblestone courtyard, the gathering crowd yapping at their feet. The air had the color and feel of late afternoon, the clear sunlight of a few hours earlier beginning to fade and tarnish. Jhalat almost ran across the courtyard and along the wall to the foot of a rickety stairway, then hauled Terek up the stairs and onto the top of the wall.

The top was broad, a good fifteen feet, with utility chambers underneath. Jhalat shoved Terek toward the outer edge. The first of the following Templemen were not far behind. As they swarmed onto the wall they gathered around and grabbed Terek and helped Jhalat drag him. Where they stopped, several heavy chains were anchored to the stones, with rusty iron rings on their free ends. The Templemen, laughing noisily and joking among themselves, grabbed Terek’s arms and legs and locked the heavy rings onto them. One stood a few feet away, right on the edge, gesturing wildly and yelling shrilly to the Wall Street marketplace below that there was a new Dunce on the wall. Others streamed up the stairs from the courtyard, carrying boxes and jars which they set down on the wall and opened up to get out the vestments. They tore Terek's clothes off and substituted an ill-fitting assortment of garishly colored rags, hanging them on him as if they were decorating a festivity bush or a parade dora. They sloshed brightly colored, sticky, strongly scented paints all over his face and body.

And all the while, merchants and townspeople were gathering in Wall Street to stare and point and laugh. Among them Terek saw neighbors and—he had thought—friends, laughing as harshly as anyone else.

Two Templemen were taking something large and heavy from a box—the helmet, a huge, bizarre thing of metal and wood and dora antlers. One standing on each side, they lifted it high over Terek's head, the others moving aside to make room for them. Then they lowered it onto his head, and the crowd—Templemen on the wall and townspeople in the street alike—erupted in a long, loud, sarcastic cheer accompanied by stomping and clapping. One Templeman put a small dish of water on the wall by one of the chain anchors and then drew quickly back.

And Terek stared, at the Templemen and the throng below. The weight of the helmet was almost staggering, and the intended humiliation extreme. But he would not give them the satisfaction of looking crushed by either. Slowly, unhurriedly, he drew himself fully erect, composed his face, and stared disdainfully, letting his gaze move slowly over every individual face.

The show was over and his reaction made some of them uncomfortable. A few wandered off; others followed until no one remained in the streets. The Templemen filed back down to the courtyard and into the inner monastery. Left completely alone, Terek sank dejectedly to the pavement—through the chains would not let him find anything like a comfortable position—and stared vacantly off at the western horizon.

There the sky, deep blue directly overhead, was beginning

to flame red with impending night. Clouds were gathering that could bring rain before morning, and Terek wondered, almost without hope, whether his work would ever again have a chance.

9

They had an alarm set for slightly before dawn, but Chet woke up even earlier. The small stateroom was still dark—not, of course, because the sun wasn't up yet, since there was no way to see the outside from here, but simply because the alarm circuits had barely begun the slow increase in illumination which preceded the actual alarm chimes. There was still little enough ambient light so that the soft green glow of controls and furniture edges stood out prominently, and barely enough for Chet to see, by looking quite closely, that Tina was still asleep.

He studied her face for a few seconds, propped up on one elbow, then eased himself back onto the mattress next to her and lay gazing toward the barely visible ceiling. There was no danger of his falling asleep again, he knew. There was too much on his mind. That was why he was awake so early in the first place.

He could hardly argue with Kel's concern about the risks involved in going into Yldac today. Previously they had gone into quite normal areas and taken pains to avoid drawing suspicion to themselves. Today everything was different. Today they were going into an area which they knew was disturbed—and they didn't know why. But they did know that the reason was very probably connected directly with them. And, by the very nature of their task, they would be more likely than ever before to attract suspicion.

It was not a particularly pleasant thought.

As he lay there in the darkness, turning it over in his mind and listening to Tina's quiet, regular breathing, Chet thought of one thing he could do about it. Taking care to be quiet and disturb the double bed as little as possible, he stood up and started to open the door. Tina stirred slightly but didn't wake up. As soon as she had settled back, Chet opened the door, slipped out quickly, and closed it again.

The corridor was a little more brightly lighted than the stateroom, but not much. Chet paused for a few seconds between the door he had just come out of and the one to the stateroom Jem Wadkinz and Bydron Kel shared, then went forward. Passing between Stiv's quarters and the galley, he emerged into the fore cabin, with PFSU and control consoles a muted galaxy of soft multicolored glows in the darkness. He went directly to the control console, sat down in the pilot's seat, and made a series of adjustments on the communications test unit. As he worked, he glanced up at the viewing panel that still showed the outside world; the eastern sky was just beginning to lighten.

As soon as the test unit was set, Chet flicked his tongue sideways. A small needle on the panel jumped into a green arc. He moved his tongue again, slightly, and the needle dropped back to rest. A still small voice inside his head said, "This is a test. If there is any—"

A final flick of his tongue and the voice went silent. Chet stood up, satisfied. He hadn't expected anything to be wrong, but this was no time to take chances. The rudimentary transceiver he carried in a second molar would be their only link with the landing boat today, and a link might be crucial.

He had already gone several steps aft when it occurred to him that there was something else he should do, and he would just as soon do it while no one else was around to listen. He went back to the console and switched on the main communicator to call Ben Jonz aboard the orbiting mother ship.

The call signal sounded a long time before he got an answer, and then Ben's voice was tired and annoyed. "What is it?" he mumbled.

"Sorry, Ben." Chet spoke quietly, his hand cupped around the microphone to minimize any slight chance of being overheard by anyone who happened to have a stateroom door open. "Chet here. You were asleep, I guess."

"Of course I was," Ben said with obvious restraint. "What's up?"

"Trouble, probably. We're still at Yldac. Tina found some funny stuff on the PFSU after our show here. We're afraid we've been discovered."

"Hm-m-m. How bad?"

"That's what we have to find out. But it doesn't look good so far. It looks like the Temple's involved."

"Oh." Ben sounded suddenly more wide awake. "Oh. Well, what can I do to help?"

"Maybe nothing. Maybe you can give us some information or advice. Maybe there's something that's obvious to you up there that we can't see because we're too close to it. I just wanted to tell you why we're still here and what we plan to do. If you have any special words of wisdom for us, that'll be just fine."

"Okay. Shoot."

"We're going into town at dawn to try to find out what's up. It'll mean going places and doing things we like to avoid, and we could get into trouble. We may wind up depending on Stiv to get us out, so you keep your thinker working in case he needs help."

"Okay. I can't really think of anything to suggest, except be careful. And—oh, yes. It just occurred to me that if you should get delayed very long you might have to worry about the other thing I was going to tell you about later today."

Chet stiffened. "What's that?"

"Ketaxil," said Ben. "I don't have enough resolution from up here to be sure, but somebody is moving around down there. From what I know about things, Ketaxil are my best guess. Headed your way."

Chet nodded grimly. The possibility of their path crossing that of Ketaxil raiders had seemed fairly remote, but it was the main reason they had had Jonz continually scanning the surface. The timing could hardly have been worse. At any stop before this one, the BEL party could have simply moved out in time to avoid a confrontation. Here, now, that was out of the question. Their only hope was time.

"Figures." Chet said quietly. "When will they get here?"

"Hard to say," said Ben. "Their movements are kind of erratic. I hadn't mentioned it before because they hadn't done anything consistent enough to establish a trend I could extrapolate with any confidence, and they didn't seem close enough to worry about unless they did. But now . . . let's see. I'd guess that if Yldac is actually their target and they really push from where they are now, they could make it in a day or so. Or it could be a week, or they could be headed somewhere else. But it wouldn't be a good idea to count on that. And of course, I can't give you much of an idea of how strong a force it is."

"If you see it from up there." Chet observed, "it's not to be trifled with. Thanks for warning me, Ben . . . and please don't say anything about this to the others unless you have to. But keep an eye on it. We're not carrying any communication gear today except my tooth radio, but we can keep in touch through Stiv and the boat radio."

"Will do. Good luck."

Chet switched off. Returning slowly along the corridor to his cabin, he mulled over the situation. Getting cut off from the landing boat at the time of a Ketaxil attack could be disastrous. It would be most desirable to have more specific knowledge than Ben could provide about where the Ketaxil were and what they were doing—*before* going in to check on the PFSU indications.

He toyed briefly with the idea of lifting the boat for a better look—taking off, getting a location from Ben, and buzzing the place at low altitude. The boat's quiet operation and external invisibility made the idea almost completely safe, as far as the Ketaxil were concerned. But Stiv would have to carry out the maneuver, and Kel would insist on knowing why. . . .

Chet had a strong hunch that it would be best not even to tell him about any of this until absolutely necessary. A hunch that he and Tina and Jem were more likely to make a good decision in a real emergency than Kel was under the remote threat of one. So, decisively and without further deliberation, he thrust the idea of an airborne scouting expedition out of his mind.

Tina was awake when he got back to their stateroom. She had turned the lights up, though not to a full daytime level, and was sitting on the edge of the bed getting dressed. "Morning," she said as he came in and sat down beside her. "Where have you been?"

"Fore cabin," he said, starting to gather his costume for the day. "Checking my tooth transceiver. Wouldn't want to take any chances on it today."

"No," Tina agreed. "Was something wrong? You were gone quite a while."

"No," said Chet. "Nothing wrong. Guess I'm just slow." He hesitated. It didn't seem quite honest to stop there, and he and Tina were always honest with each other. Yet he hated to raise fears which might not be necessary. . . .
But they might. And Tina was quite capable of handling them. "There is one other thing," he admitted. "But don't mention it in front of Agent Bydron. . . ."

Restricting themselves to Chet's tooth radio instead of the more reliable pocket sets they usually carried was just one part of an attempt to carry as few traces of their parent civilization as possible. The possibility of being taken into custody and searched by natives was one they didn't like to think about, but couldn't afford to ignore. Obviously they couldn't hope to withstand a really determined search—one that went beyond the clothes they wore—but they could certainly avoid conspicuous objects like communicators and weapons. And they could minimize the likelihood of a thorough search by showing as little as possible that could conceivably arouse suspicions. So, for example, the outfit with which Tina had shocked Kel before their first show was out. Today she appeared in a hooded cloak, generally similar to the colorful robes Chet and Jem wore, but leaving little more than her face exposed.

The designs were as authentic and as meticulously done as those they had used before. Even so, this morning they felt painfully conspicuous and vulnerable as they walked down the ramp, and even more so when the ramp swung up and the boat disappeared, leaving them alone with the morning.

They had never been out this early before. The air still had a chill in it, such direct sunlight as reached them was ruddy, and big beads of dew stood on the round-leaved grass in the clearing and the high shrubbery that pressed in on them from all sides. The thicket, a twisted, nearly impenetrable tangle vaguely resembling rhododendrons with thorns, made the clearing one of the best landing sites they had found. Natives seldom ventured into the troublesome snarl. But, by the same token, getting out was no picnic.

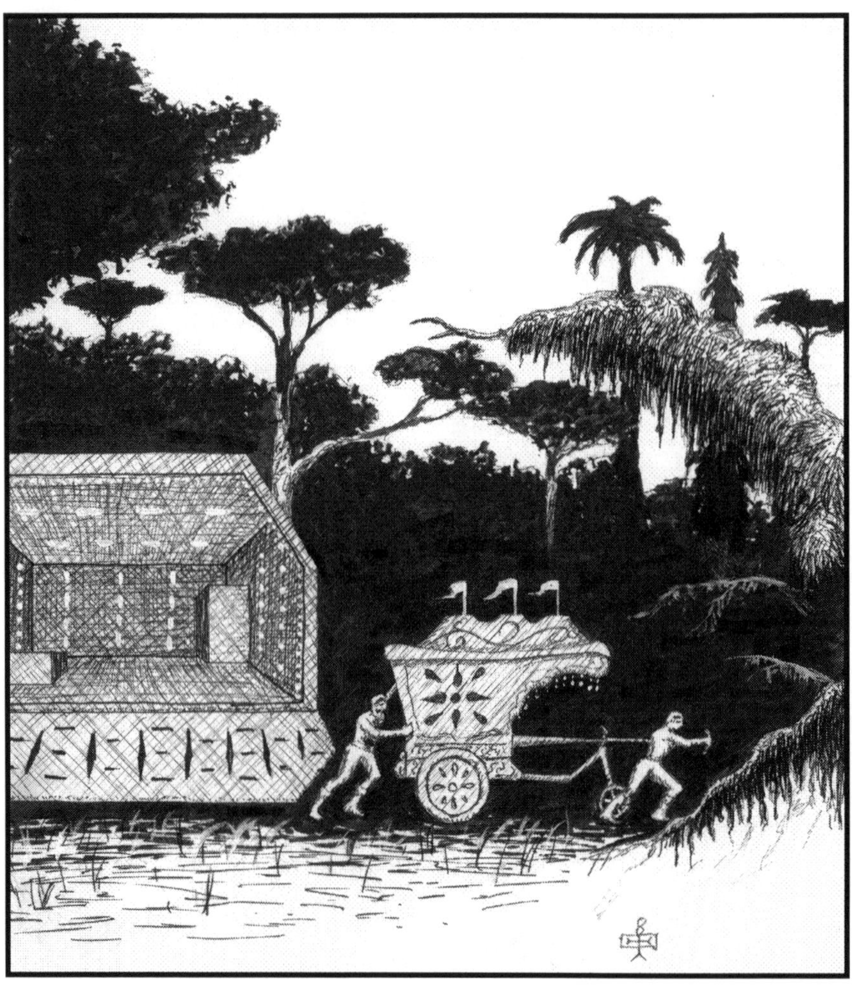

Chet, Tina, and Jem threaded their way among the grasping thorns with delicate care to avoid damage to their costumes, and the going was neither fast nor easy. Only Jem, for the first time without the cart, found any cause for rejoicing.

The barrier was a half mile thick. They stopped at its edge, just inside the protective cover, both to rest from the exertion of getting through the bush and to survey the thousand yards of open plain between them and the town for any sign of imminent danger. The PFSU could do little more than raise suspicions and doubts, but it had done that very effectively. And they were acutely aware that if any trouble arose, they would be able to do little more than call Sandor and Kel and hope for help.

From here, no danger was apparent. The sight, except for minor variations, was thoroughly familiar to them by now. Yldac rose from the plain directly ahead, with the same outstanding features as every other Kengmor town they had seen. The same outermost rim of low, dingy houses of rough-hewn wood, with thick smoke billowing from tall thin chimneys . . . the same terraced central mountain of the monastery, capped by the dixar's castle. . . .

The surrounding plain, flatter than some they had seen, showed little evidence of deliberate road-making. But tiny farmhouses, rather like those of the periphery, sprinkled the plain, and the careful eye could even pick up traces of paths linking them. Moving out of the bush with an unusually high level of caution and wariness, Jem and the Barlins started across, following those faint traces at maximum distance from the farmhouses whenever possible.

A few farmers were out already, but only a few. The pastoral scenes, like the towns, had taken on a definite air of familiarity. A farmer, still clothed warmly against the chill of autumn dawn, pushed his plow behind a dora. Another carried a basket among his flock of waist-high xarlol, picking off their tails and other seemingly ornamental appendages to be cooked into rich stews. The process had seemed startlingly cruel to the humans until they realized that the sad-faced animals regenerated as easily as lizards or earthworms. Now, accustomed to the practice, they hardly took notice of Kemrekl raising them like cattle and harvesting them like fruit trees.

Far off to the left, one of the farmhouses stood abandoned, half collapsed and rotting, at the very edge of the water that had not been there a few years earlier. Next to it stood a cannon installation, much like the one they had noticed on the way to their first show at Yxyngar—even to the nest in the muzzle, though this nest's occupants had apparently already left for winter quarters. Since Yxyngar, the Barlins had learned that such installations were common. Every town had at least one or two pointing out over the water to remind prowling Ketaxil that they were unwelcome—and most of them were as ill-kept as this one and the one at Yxyngar. Looking at this one brought this morning's disquieting conversation with Ben Jonz vividly back into Chet's mind. He found himself thinking involuntarily of how much more complicated things could get before they left this place.

So far the island towns had consistently succeeded in repelling the pirates from their shores, although boats sent out from the towns to face them on their own ground—the water—were rarely heard from again. But those cannons were old and primitive. There had been rumor in the towns, since before Chet and Tina first set foot in Yngmor, that the Ketaxil were developing improved weapons and tactics.

And now Ben thought he had direct evidence that another attack might be imminently possible. It was right here in Yldac, Chet remembered too well, that he and Tina had once before seen such an attack at close range—the one which had finally driven them back to Larneg for permission to intervene.

The memory of that one was burned indelibly into both their minds. *If the next one came today,* Chet wondered grimly, *would the old defenses be adequate to repel it?*

The periphery had an air about it. The Temple supported and encouraged many kinds of studies, but none directed toward such crassly practical goals as inside plumbing or odorless garbage disposal. As a result, even though the narrow packed-dirt streets that wound among the close-packed shacks were now relatively empty, the humans' noses brought them ample reminders that the area was densely populated. Only a few of the residents were in the streets this early—mostly housekeepers fetching water from community wells, keeping their distance and stealing shy glances at the foreigners. But the others were there, Chet and Tina knew well, behind the small, tightly shuttered windows in the shacks. And it seemed to them that all the thousands of eyes along the street and hidden behind chinks in the walls must be staring at them.

Intellectually, Chet knew that was highly unlikely, but the awareness that suspicions had likely been aroused made him unusually wary. He could see something similar in Tina's face, although she hid it so well that anyone not married to her would have missed it. Wadkinz's anxiety, in contrast, was painfully obvious.

They hurried through, talking little and pressing on toward the structure that loomed over the whole town. On another day, they might have paused before one of the few shacks that had an ornamental strip of flowers planted beside the door; today they didn't even consider it. When they passed a townsperson on foot—and they passed more and more as the hour grew later and they approached the center of town—they made as much effort as he did to pass at a good distance. They passed a neighborhood garbage dump where a shackled dora and half a dozen lytangl—sharp-faced animals vaguely resembling dogs, but covered with yellowish scales and plates more reptilian than mammalian—feasted on civilization's castoffs. The lytangl looked up as the humans approached, staring pointedly and making rasping sounds in their throats. Chet led Tina and Jem well clear of the pack, thinking wryly as he did so that he even seemed to feel the suspicion in the scavengers' gaze.

Calm down, boy, he told himself sternly. *Nothing's happened yet—and you know they're not in on it. Don't you?*

Despite his deliberate efforts to control it, the edgy feeling intensified when they reached the monastery. They paused in the shadows between two buildings at the end of one of the little radial streets, hesitating before stepping out into the wide openness of Wall Street. Across the street rose the gray stone wall of the monastery itself, so close that it blocked their view of everything beyond except the very pinnacle where the dixar lived. So far nothing had happened, but there would be other eyes behind the small windows high in this wall—and some of those eyes were far more likely to represent real threats than any in the periphery. Yet, precisely for that reason—because the PFSU had said that the recent unusual activity was centered here—this was where they had to come.

"I don't really know what we're looking for," Chet said in Anglarneg, "but this is probably as close as we can get to it right now." He glanced up at the pointed turret jutting above the wall, far beyond it. "Not that I'm complaining, yet. If you have any better ideas, Tina, speak up, but my hunch is that we might as well just wander around the wall with our eyes and ears open. If anybody outside the inner sanctum knows anything, the marketplace ought to be a good place to pick it up. What do you think?"

"That's about how I figured," Tina nodded. "Separately or together?"

"Together," Chet said at once. "I can't think of a single advantage of splitting up—except the slight possibility that one of us might get into trouble and another could get away. But remember, I'm the only one with a radio." He turned to Wadkinz. "Jem?"

The quasimaterials specialist shrugged. "You're the boss."

They stepped out into Wall Street, the cobblestones strikingly solid underfoot after the dirt streets of the periphery. The smells here were more pleasant—the day's customers were just beginning to converse on the market, but the merchants had started setting up their wares even before sunrise, and the air was rich with the scents of meat and vegetables and fish and flowers. Along one side of the broad street ran the monastery wall, drab and nearly featureless except for the small windows near the top and the big reinforced doors spaced at long intervals along the base. The market lined the other side, a noisy, varied panorama of Kengmor life. Skilled artisans sold blankets, utensils, clothing, candles, and icons in permanent shops with elegant pictographic signs proclaiming their wares. One of the shops, with a particularly elaborate sign in front, specialized in the signs for other shops, at prices so high as to be baffling. Some of them were taverns of sorts, quieter now than on some evenings Chet could remember, but already doing a lively business among both shoppers and merchants. Interspersed among the solid-walled and roofed shops were dozens of impromptu, casually tented stalls where farmers and others from outlying areas sold firewood, sleeping straw, and all the products of agriculture. Haggling, though present everywhere, was loudest here. A growing throng of shoppers and farmers driving dora carts circulated continuously among the stalls and shops. Splinters of a hundred conversations drifted to Chet's ears and then moved off. None seemed to have anything to do with his problem.

Surrounded by vegetable stands with little to offer but the grain tyraxet, a butcher loudly shouted the excellence of his meats, hanging above the counter amid buzzing swarms of airborne arthropods. Townspeople approached his stall with a mixture of eagerness and apprehension. Meat was scarce these days—livestock does not use land as efficiently as tyraxet, and land was at a premium since the Shakes—but the taste had not been lost. There were not many butchers in the market, and perhaps this one would have more reasonable prices than the others. . . .

But he didn't. Prospective customers came, drooled, tried to haggle, and went away disappointed. The butcher watched them go with equal frustration. To break even, he *had* to charge those prices, but if people wouldn't pay them, what could he do?

In the next stall, a rough-voiced man whose beard and accent marked him as foreign tried to outshout the butcher and entice his disappointed customers to try his seafoods—small streamlined things rather like sharks, conical shellfish with pink tentacles, and an assortment of slimy things in crystalline jars. People hesitated and looked—his prices were tempting and his food said to be nutritious—and then went on without buying. Before the Shakes, such things had been disdained as food by the people of the towns. Slowly, they were beginning to be accepted, but the taste was still far from widespread.

Chet toyed briefly with the idea of trying to strike up a conversation with the fishmonger, to ask him such things as where he lived and how long he had been coming here. Did he routinely travel the waterways? If so, how did he avoid trouble with the Ketaxil? The answers could have been valuable. But speaking to anyone at this point could well prove more dangerous than just listening. So, after a moment's hesitation, Chet dropped the idea, at least for now.

Like a comparable marketplace in at least half of the comparable cultures Chet knew, this one was not without its quota of beggars and itinerant entertainers, all trying in their own ways to get the little ceramic coins from anyone who would part with them. They had almost passed one of the entertainers, a lithe young girl with a juggling act, when Jem stopped, did a double take, and tugged at Chet's arm. "Did you see that?" he whispered.

Chet and Tina both looked back at the juggler. She was good, but at first they didn't see exactly what had caught Jem's eye. Then Chet notice a couple of objects the girl was juggling—first their odd behavior, and then their familiar appearance. He blinked. "Are those what I think they are?"

Tina grinned. "I'm sure of it. And I ought to know—she

bought them from me."

Jem nodded. "Yep. Quasimaterials. That gal picked up some of your samples after the show and worked them into her own act."

"And pretty deftly, too," Chet noted approvingly. "She's taking advantage of their peculiarities, all right, but they don't seem to bother her."

"Or the audience." Tina pursed her lips and frowned. "It's maddening, Chet. Like Kel said, they're typical. Quasimaterials don't faze them at all—mostly. But *somebody's* really upset. Where is he? We've come almost all the way around the monastery and we still haven't found anything like what we saw on the PFSU."

Once around Monastery Wall Street amounted to just under a mile. When they got back to the junction with the side street by which they had entered, Chet stopped, frowning. "Nothing," he muttered, "Now what?"

"I suppose," Wadkinz mused, "Kel would say that proves there's no problem and we should go back to the boat and be on our way as if you'd never seen anything on the PFSU. But I have a hunch you're not going to buy that."

"You bet we're not," said Tina. "I *did* see something."

"We're pretty sure it's in there," Chet said, gesturing at the forbidding wall across the street. "We hoped we might find some evidence of it out here, and we didn't. All that proves is that it's still in there rather than out here. And that, I'm afraid, mean it's going to be a lot harder to get at then we'd hoped. But we still need to get at it."

They all stood silent for many seconds. None of them was anxious to suggest that they were going to have to start thinking about a way to find out exactly what was going on inside the monastery. The only way that seemed anything like obvious was to somehow *go* inside. . . .

"Maybe we could plant a bug on a Templeman," Chet said finally. "But I don't like to think about doing that either." He paused, then said, "I can think of one more thing we can try out here—other than just walking around again."

Tina asked the obvious question with her eyes.

"Let's go into a tavern for a while," said Chet, "and just sit and listen. There's one just a few steps back, and it should be as good a place for gossip as we're going to find."

The tavern's sign featured a relief caricature of a lytang gazing morosely into a huge two-handled-mug—a recognizable attempt at humor in a society where such things were notably scarce. They entered through a low door covered with a fringe of yielding vegetable fibers. The room beyond was dark, windowless and lit only by the phosphorescent fungi on the walls and the elaborate, individually shaped candles on the tables, all of which were burning whether the table was occupied or not. There were a dozen or so of the small round tables, scattered around the room apparently at random. Each table was surrounded by three or four low stools carved from sections of log from a non-local tree. Chet estimated that about a third of the available seats were occupied, by natives in a variety of postures and moods ranging from noisy elation to melancholy meditation. But without exceptions, each patron had one of the two-handled mugs, either raised to his mouth or standing ready on the table before him.

"I suppose we'll be expected to buy some mrebhev," Chet sighed. "The things we do in the line of duty!"

There was a raised platform in each rear corner of the tavern. The one on the right harbored a couple playing a sort of bone flute and a three-stringed plectrum instrument which, to Larnegites, sounded badly in need of tuning. The one of the left, toward which Chet's party headed, held a single huge barrel with a rotund villager seated on one of the stools next to it. He looked up at their approach, then reached behind him and pulled three of the mugs out of a tub which Chet knew doubled as storage bin and disinfectant vat. By the time they got close enough to talk to him, the bartender had filled two of the mugs from a spigot on the side of the barrel, and was just topping off the third.

One of the advantages of a simple menu, I suppose, Chet thought as he fished two of the coins they had earned at magic shows out of his outfit and dropped them in the slot-topped basket at the bartender's feet. The bartender nodded slightly, handed him one of the mugs, and muttered a Lingmor word meaning something like "Skoal!" Then he repeated the ritual with Jem and finally with Tina. It was essential, of course, that Tina go last and that each pay for his or her own drink. Anything else would have been a conspicuous, unpardonable, and potentially dangerous breach of etiquette.

Chet led them through the darkness, casting about for a table. Peace of mind dictated a corner table as far from anyone else as possible. Their reason for being here dictated exactly the opposite. So Chet led them unhesitatingly to a table in the middle of the room, with near neighbors on almost every side.

They all sat staring at the bubbly froth in their mugs, sampling the conversations at neighboring tables and putting off the first sip as long as they conveniently could. In Kemrekl, mrebhev produced various kinds of intoxication, most of them represented among the tavern's present customers and practically all of them regarded as pleasant. The active ingredient had not yet been identified by human investigators, but in human drinkers it produced nothing except a taste faintly suggestive of a mixture of soap and gasoline and an unpleasant tickling in the throat that sometimes lasted for hours.

While conditioning himself against the taste, Chet heard two farmers to his left talking about the troubles they'd been having with a root parasite. He tuned that out and tried another table. Directly behind him, somebody said, "Say, did you see the Dunce?"

Another said, "No, my stall's on the other side of the monastery, and I figure if you've seen one Dunce you've seem them all. I saw one once." They both laughed.

It didn't occur to any of them until later that that was the conversation they should have followed. The key word was vaguely familiar to both the Barlins, but its significance failed to register.

And all their attentions at once latched tenaciously onto another key word that came from a table behind Tina. The word was "Ketaxil."

Chet lifted his mug and, being very careful to be quiet, pretended to drink. The big fellow who had mentioned Ketaxil—in a voice conveniently loud, if a bit slurry at the moment—was saying, "I tell you they'll be back. And when they come back, it's not going to be the same as before. They're brewing new tricks. It's going to be bad for us, I tell you."

"What kind of new tricks, Lelar?" his companion asked dreamily. To Chet, it was fairly obvious that she didn't particularly care, but was quite willing to converse amiably on any subject at all.

"New weapons," the big man bellowed. "Like"—and here his voice became overbearingly confidential—"a tame dragon. A giant tame dragon that breathes fire on whoever they tell it to."

Chet and Tina glanced at each other, both wondering the same thing. Was this pure intoxicated fantasy or did it possibly have some basis in fact? They were depending heavily on the fact that none of the natives knew the whole planet too well—but neither did they. Any planet worth the name is too big and wondrously varied to pretend to know after a few weeks' acquaintance. For all Chet *knew*, something very much like the man's description might actually exist on Ymrek, and the Ketaxil might even have learned to control it. Or, more likely, the report might be a grossly garbled and embellished version of something more mundane but at least as deadly. Or. . . .

"That's fascinating, Lelar," the blustery man's dreamy-voiced companion said soothingly. "Where did you find out about the tame dragon?"

"From the outlanders," Lelar told her. "They've been out there among them. They *know*."

Hm-m-m, Chet thought. *What outlanders?* It could well be that he himself was one of them—that the Barlins' magic troupe had been found a conveniently authoritative and uncheckable source to attribute the latest flight of fancy to. On the other hand, other foreigners did come occasionally, and not always with pomp and ceremony. Chet remembered the fishmonger he had wanted to talk to. . . .

They listened a few minutes longer. Chet grew more and more doubtful that this conversation really contained anything of significance. When he finally ventured to take a real sip of his mrebhev, he lost the last of his patience.

"We're not going to get anything here," he said in Anglarneg, standing up. "Might as well go outside. Take one more stroll around Wall Street, and if we still haven't found anything, we'll just have to go back to the boat and try to think of something else."

So they went back out, pausing at the door to readjust to sunlight and then started around the monastery again.

And this time they saw the Dunce.

Chet didn't recognize the grotesque figure's significance at first, but that in itself was cause for suspicion. "Look up there!" he whispered, stopping and pointing. "Up on the wall. What's with him?"

Tina and Jem looked. The wall was ten or twelve feet high, and now a native, barely recognizable in garish paint and clothes, stood at the edge some hundred feet ahead. He wore a huge, bizarre helmet and there were chains on his elbows and wrists, but he was standing very erect and looking this way.

Tina frowned for a second, then nodded with sudden recognition. "A Dunce," she said. "Remember we heard somebody ask about one in the tavern? It bounced right off me at the time, but now I remember what it means." Chet remembered, too, now, but Tina went on to explain for Jem. "A Dunce is a minor heretic. The Temple doesn't tolerate ideas too much unlike its own, of course. But the priests know better than to execute anybody, except as an extreme last resort. Martyrs are so awkward—if you kill somebody for his ideas, it strongly suggests you took them seriously. The Temple prefers to nip heresy in the bud by holding the troublemaker up to public ridicule. So they stand him out on the monastery wall in a clown suit and—" She broke off suddenly and Chet could see her mind racing. "Chet!" she squealed. "Could he be it? If we have something to do with his heresy—"

Before Chet could answer, the Dunce called to them. At first they weren't quite sure, but then he repeated the call and no doubt could remain.

Startled, Tina looked at Chet. "Maybe I was right. He wants us to come. Should we?"

"Sounds dangerous to me," Wadkinz grunted.

Chet had a disquieting suspicion that Jem was right. But he nodded anyway. "I think we'd better," he said.

They went.

At close range, they saw that the Dunce was smiling with a surprising air of calm confidence. Looking down from his high perch, he gave an uncomfortable impression of considering himself in command of the situation. He stared at them silently for some seconds and then asked, "Where do you come from?"

Chet suddenly became very apprehensive. The question had been anticipated, of course, and he gave the stock answer. But he had a feeling it wouldn't satisfy this customer. "We have traveled far," he said, "from a distant land where—"

"Where?" the Dunce interrupted bluntly.

Chet didn't bother to finish the rehearsed answer. And he knew he was on much more treacherous ground ad-libbing. "You wouldn't know the place," he said. "No one from Yngmor has ever been there."

"I can believe that," the Dunce said. He made it sound as if it had more than surface meaning. "Do you recognize me?"

Evidently Tina's guess had not been too far wrong. "I'm not sure," Chet said. "Should I?"

"I would hope so," the Dunce said wryly. "It's the least you could do after the way you wrecked my life."

Chet blinked. "Wrecked your life? Us? How's that?"

"I was at your show yesterday," the Dunce said. "It was the best I've ever seen. That's the trouble—it was too good. It destroyed everything I had done toward getting the blessing of the Temple for my work. But my work's *right*, your tricks notwithstanding! So I hoped you'd come back. I hoped to persuade you to help me unwreck my life—to placate the dixar Kangyr—"

Chet was beginning to see where the Dunce fitted into yesterday's incident—and implications of something possibly much bigger behind that. But before the Dunce finished explaining, they were interrupted by a clatter of rapidly approaching footsteps and a harsh voice. "Hey, you, there! What are you doing?"

Chet turned to see the Templeman running toward them with ceremonial lance raised and instantly recognized potential trouble. He foresaw, for instance, the likelihood of a forced separation from the figure who seemed to be the key to what Tina had seen on the PFSU. He turned quickly back to the Dunce. "For future reference," he said, "what's your name?"

"Terek," said Terek.

The Templeman halted, puffing, a lance length away from Chet. "Why were you talking to the prisoner?" he demanded.

"What difference does it make?" Tina taunted. "He's just a Dunce." She glanced up at Terek and added, "No offense."

"None taken," Terek said. Then, to the Templeman, "These are the so-called magicians who got me into this mess, Xymrok."

Xymrok lifted his lance tip momentarily in a perfunctory threatening gesture. "You know better than to address a Templeman by name," he muttered. Then he looked puzzled—or so Chet thought, although there were enough differences between human and Kemrek facial expressions that he couldn't always be sure. "If that's true," Xymrok mused, "why should they be talking to you?'

"He called us," Chet said. "We didn't know—"

Xymrok looked up. "That so?"

"You have the outlander's word," Terek said dryly. "Of course I did. I don't especially like it up here, and I had plenty of time to think about it during the night. I thought if they would talk to Kangyr—"

"*The dixar* Kangyr!" Xymrok corrected sharply. He frowned. "None of you are making any sense, but this all smells very funny. I've half a mind to haul you up to the dixar on suspicion, but I'm not sure it's worth his trouble."

"Look at their hands," Terek suggested.

Wadkinz turned white; Chet and Tina just quietly abandoned any remaining hope of evading discovery. The Templeman looked, at first uncomprehendingly, then with widening eyes as he counted only five fingers on hand after hand.

Then he looked up at Chet, all traces of indecision gone from his face. "Come along," he said.

And as he herded them toward the nearest door, Chet muttered in Anglarneg, "Well, folks, I'm reminded of an old sign that used to proliferate along roadsides in one of our ancestral cultures, back on Earth around the beginning of space travel."

"What's that?" Jem asked tensely.

Chet grinned wryly, without real humor. "Prepare to meet God."

10

From the standpoint of either xenologist or comparative historian, the opportunity was splendid, of course. Their knowledge of the Temple had so far been based entirely on indirect findings—PFSU readings, remote eavesdropping with scopes and paramikes, discreet conversations with natives who might occasionally have some knowledge of the religion which ruled them. Much of what the Barlins would have liked to learn lay solidly locked within monastery walls. A firsthand look inside a monastery was more then they had ever dared hope for.

However, neither Chet nor Tina had ever met anyone who considered being arrested by their subjects a recommended research method. Which made their situation hard to fully appreciate.

Jem's position was even worse. No doubt he could see little to recommend being taken inside, and he was even more in the dark than Chet and Tina about just what was going on. The whole conversation with Terek and the Templeman might just as well have been Sanskrit, for all the good it did him. And there was no chance to explain. . . .

The door was big and plain, the knocker an icon of Kangyr. It opened promptly in response to Xymrok's signal; the space beyond was dark and damp-smelling. Another Templeman stepped into view from within; he and Xymrok exchanged a few brief words. Then the guard stepped aside and Xymrok nudged the humans into the darkness with the side of his lance. The guard eased the door shut and it took the day with it.

They stood for a few seconds, letting their eyes adjust to

the mixture of torchlight and thin shafts of daylight from the windows high in the outer wall. Xymrok prodded them impatiently and they went ahead of him along a lengthy stretch and around a corner. Chet wondered briefly whether now was the time to call Stiv with his tooth transceiver, and decided against it.

Just as their dark adaptation had become good enough to be sure there was little to see in the corridor within the wall, Xymrok scooted ahead of them and flung a new door open to bright daylight. He led them out briefly, cutting across a corner of a cobblestone courtyard, right past a substructure which Chet suddenly realized must be one of the chapels they had previously seen only from the air. He hadn't realized they were so heavily ornamented. A couple of olive-robed Templeman strolled by, ignoring them and chatting contentedly about some philosophical matter. . . .

And then back into the darkness, this time into a short black tunnel which dipped abruptly—they splashed through a puddle at the bottom—and then rose into a new corridor, drier and better lit than the first, and with a slightly different musty aroma. It proved the first of many; Xymrok led them briskly along such corridors, up long winding staircases, and along more corridors, only occasionally meeting a Templeman or a Disciple. The icons were everywhere, and here and there they passed alcoves containing displays of art objects or relics of miracles displaying the magnificent variability of the Ways. Chet would have very much liked a closer look at any of them, and he knew Tina would have, too. But of course that was out of the question. . . .

They arrived finally at the top of a stairway which opened into nothing except a single short corridor with a guard at the end. Xymrok stomped ahead of them toward the door, banging the butt of his lance on the floor like a cane, moving briskly and showing no inclination to slow up. The Templeman guarding the door seemed to recognize him and moved at once to open the door. Xymrok went in with unbroken stride and beckoned impatiently for them to follow.

And there they were. The fact had barely had time to register on Chet's consciousness when he realized that Xymrok had shifted his lance to his other hand and was performing the salute reserved for only one man in any town—if man was the word. The humans knew about the salute and had a general idea of how it was done—but not much faith in their sources. A bit frantically, Chet watched Xymrok and tried to mimic as exactly as possible what he had done. Out of the corners of his eyes he saw Tina and Jem doing likewise.

To his considerable relief, the purple-robed native at the far end of the long table returned the salute. He was old, Chet observed, and looked a good deal like a beardless gnome. The icons—including the ones in this room—flattered him.

When he had finished the ritual greeting, he looked expectantly at Xymrok. He said nothing.

"These are said to be the magicians whose performance led to Terek's disgrace yesterday, Your Holiness," Xymrok explained. "They were found talking to Terek and could not explain themselves to my satisfaction." He paused briefly and added, "I suggest also that Your Holiness examine their hands."

The dixar Kangyr glanced quickly at their hands, and his forehead wrinkled almost imperceptibly. "Magnificent and infinitely varied are the ways of the Supreme Presence," he recited indifferently. "Xymrok, you may leave the room."

Xymrok saluted and left, closing the big wooden door quietly behind him. Kangyr affected something resembling a very relaxed smile. "I don't suppose you'd like to tell me where you're from?"

"It would be difficult, Your Holiness," Chet said warily. "It's a very distant land—"

Kangyr dismissed the thought with a wave of his hand before Chet finished. "No matter. There is surely room in the world for a land of people with five fingers, and surely the Supreme Presence would find it no great challenge to create such a people. Is it true that you were talking to Terek?"

"I suppose it is," Chet said. He added cautiously, "If that's who the Dunce was."

Kangyr's eyebrows rose slightly again. "You don't know him?"

"No."

"Then why were you talking to him?"

"He called us."

"Why?"

The question caught Chet slightly off guard. "We didn't really have time to find out, Your Holiness. The Templeman Xymrok interrupted us and brought us here before we had heard enough of what the Dunce had to say to actually understand it."

"I see," said the dixar. He leaned on one elbow, cradling his chin in a big hand. "A pity, perhaps—but it's done. I wonder . . . how did you happen to be so near Terek that he was able to call out to you from the wall?"

"What?" Chet didn't like this character's manner of questioning—he hit too many unexpected weak points that should have been thought out better than they had been. "We were merely walking in the marketplace—"

"A bit odd," Kangyr interrupted. "Many of the show people who visit Yldac seem to shy away from the marketplace. They seem to want to keep very much to themselves. Yet you just happened to be strolling there, a few yards from Terek, a few hours after you gave the show which is indirectly responsible for his present predicament. A most interesting coincidence."

"Most interesting, Your Holiness," Chet agreed. *There's something here, all right,* he thought tightly. *But I don't see what yet. And we're going to have to watch this guy like a hawk.* He said, "But I'm afraid I don't quite understand what Your Holiness is driving at. Travelers must eat and drink, too. And sometimes we simply like to see how people live in the lands we visit—"

"Yes, of course." Kangyr cut him off with another wave of his hand. "Possibly no significance to it at all. You say Terek called you and was trying to tell you something. What did he tell you?"

"As I said, I'm not sure, since he didn't finish. He said something, about our show having jeopardized his standing with the Temple, but we couldn't understand it. Your Holiness"—and Chet hoped as he said this that he wasn't going too far beyond the bounds of propriety—"could you explain to us any of what's going on and where we fit into it? We meant no harm."

Kangyr nodded slightly. "And you did none." He stared distantly at one of the icons on the wall. "Terek has strange ideas—dangerous ideas. In essence, he tried to condense all the magnificent and infinitely variable complexity of the Supreme Presence into a few simple sayings—some of them clearly and flagrantly wrong, others simply claiming to impose restrictions on the Supreme Presence where there is clearly no need for the Supreme Presence to be restricted at all." He reached down, to some drawer or table out of sight under his throne, and came back up with something in his hand. "I suppose you recognize these?"

He opened his hand. Chet had prepared himself well enough so that he didn't even blink at the sight of the two quasimaterial balls. Neither did Tina, but Jem's discomfort was obvious—and being fed constantly by his inability to follow the conversation.

Chet nodded. "Yes, Your Holiness," he said quietly. "They're souvenirs from our show." He said no more about them, though of course he recognized them much more specifically than that. From his or Jem's standpoint, the difference between them was that, unlike ordinary "real" matter, their gravitational and inertial masses were inequivalent—in opposite ways. He wondered how Kemrekl interpreted it—if they bothered.

With an abrupt jerk of his hand, Kangyr tossed both balls into the air. "There!" he exclaimed as the first came down on the tabletop. The other was just reaching the top of its upward arc. As he watched that one curve down, he said, "Terek tried to tell us they should fall at the same rate. Can you imagine that? As if the Supreme Presence could be so cramped and inflexible that things can only fall in one way!" He paused. Superficially his face was gloating—but behind that Chet felt oddly sure that he could see a steadily eroding undercurrent of deep dissatisfaction. Almost frantically, he struggled to understand exactly why. . . .

"I suppose you see now," Kangyr said more calmly, "why I owe you a debt of gratitude on behalf of the Temple."

Chet had not quite finished assimilating it yet, and his reactions were lagging. But he thought he saw enough to be sure it was more than mildly disturbing. He took the cue and asked, "Why is that, Your Holiness?"

Kangyr was staring thoughtfully at his icon again. "There are . . . ah . . . those in the Temple who were tempted to grant some acceptance to Terek's ideas, primarily because he claimed that with some of them he could greatly improve our defense capabilities. With the Ketaxil situation deteriorating as it has been . . . well, I can forgive temptation in the weaker elements of the Temple. Yet I always felt obliged to resist Terek's heresies altogether because of their terrific religious impact. Why, he even wanted us to believe Ymrek revolves around the Day Star, when everybody knows that the Day Star and everything else revolves around Ymrek!" He looked at Chet. "So I welcomed the opportunity your show gave to denounce Terek once and for all as a Dunce. After your show it was impossible for anyone to take seriously a madman who thinks all objects must fall at the same speed and—" He broke off. "But I'm boring you. Is there anything else you want to know?"

He couldn't have been more wrong about boring Chet, and there was plenty more that he wanted to know. But he was so excited and stunned by what he had heard already that he didn't want to risk saying anything else to get them into trouble. The urgent thing now was to get back to the boat and decide what to do about it. "No, Your Holiness," said Chet. "Thank you for clarifying the situation."

"The least I could do," Kangyr said. "And I thank *you* again for what you've done for the Temple. Perhaps, through your influence, even Terek will be brought back to the Truth." He paused momentarily. "I apologize for your inconvenience, but you understand that Xymrok must be suspicious of anyone he finds talking to a dangerous prisoner. Do you have any more questions?"

"No," Chet lied.

"Very well. Since this wasn't your fault, you may go with my blessing. The guard outside the door will see to it that you have escort as far as the outer gates. Feel free to stop and examine the relics along the way."

"Thank you, Your Holiness." Chet and Tina turned to go; Jem followed. They had reached the door and were about to open it when Kangyr spoke again.

"One more thing . . . please."

They stopped. Chet and Tina turned back to the dixar. There was a note of something like pleading in his voice now that sounded odd from one in his position. "Your magic," he said. "It is . . . real?"

Chet thought, startled by the question, then said cautiously, "We have learned control of some . . . er . . . spiritual phenomena which seem to be unfamiliar in this land."

"I was just thinking," Kangyr said. "If you have magic which might be effective against the Ketaxil, we could make it worth your while. . . ."

"Uh," said Chet, increasingly anxious to get away, "I'd have to consult the spirits on that."

"Please do. And if you find a way, you will let me know?"

Chet nodded uncomfortably.

They did pause to look at a few of the relics on the way out, and found them fascinating. But they didn't devote the time to them that they might have under other circumstances.

And once they were back out on the street and unescorted, they returned to the boat as fast as they possibly could.

11

". . . So it looks to me," Chet finished, "like we've just pulled off the most horrendous piece of cultural interference in history. Now it's up to us to stick around and see if we can undo any of the damage."

He was sitting in the pilot's throne, swiveled around, and the psychological advantage that might give him had definitely been a consideration in his choice of seats. Bydron Kel was in one of the middle passengers' seats, flanked by Tina and Jem, and he looked thoroughly miserable. "What are you taking about, Barlin? I don't see—"

"You don't see what's happened?" Chet interrupted with unaccustomed impatience. "I'll say it again. We've come at one of the big turning points in their history, and by introducing a few tentative samples of quasimaterials, we've frustrated it."

"We're not all historians, Chet," Wadkinz reminded gently. "You're not ringing many bells yet—and I was there, though I couldn't understand much."

"Sorry," said Chet. "I'll try to run it by a little slower. I guess I got a little overexcited—but then I've never been in on a blunder like this before. *Nobody's* ever been in on a blunder like this before." He shook his head, still amazed and appalled. "Terek," he said earnestly, "is this culture's Newton . . . and maybe Copernicus and Galileo, too, all rolled into one. I can't be completely positive how good a job he's done, yet, but from what he and Kangyr said I'm almost willing to bet that he's worked out a fairly modern picture of the universe, together with universal gravitation and Newtonian mechanics to back it up. Now we come along and give them a look at some things that don't work that way, and the established church jumps at the chance to laugh his ideas into the ground."

Kel very deliberately ground out his cigarette, sat up straight, squared his shoulders, and looked hard at Chet. "Okay," he said. "*Why?* You seem to think there's a problem and we have to do something about it. I have to make a decision about whatever you suggest doing, and so I need to understand exactly what the problem is. Yesterday you accused me of trying to oversimplify things by looking at them in terms of human history. Okay . . . so I'm putting it straight to you now. Exactly why is this Temple so anxious to suppress Terek's work? I mean, if they're willing to take magic like quasimaterials from strangers like us, without batting an eye—why not something simple and straightforward like Newton's laws?"

Chet nodded thoughtfully. The question was a fair one. He suspected that, at heart, Kel was still hoping the problem would go away if he could ignore it. But that question deserved the benefit of the doubt; he must try to answer it conscientiously. But it wasn't an easy question. . . . "Think of human history for a start," he suggested. "Not for an explanation, but for something close enough to a parallel so you can use it for a basis to work away from. Copernicus and Galileo had some of the same kind of trouble with the Catholic Church in medieval Europe—and some of those same ideas which seem so 'straightforward' to you. The Earth going around the Sun instead of the other way around? The idea was completely unacceptable—and its local counterpart is one of Terek's ideas."

"But the Temple is quite different," Tina put in. "On medieval Earth, the points of dispute were details. Nobody denied that there were natural laws, really, even though they disagreed violently about the specific content of them. But in the Temple here, the *very concept* of natural law is heretical. The Temple's creed is such that actually very few things are really heretical. But this is. Violently and fundamentally."

Kel's assertive stand wilted slightly. He lit up a new cigarette. "I guess you'd better explain," he said.

"It's not easy," Tina warned. "You know the First Precept, I assume. 'Magnificent and infinitely varied are the ways of the Supreme Presence.'"

Kel nodded. "Yes. A trite platitude that might have been mouthed by a mediocre priest of any religion in human history."

"Wrong," said Tina. "Sure, something similar might have been used that way thousands of times. But here it's the *First Precept*, and you can't hope to understand until you fully grasp that. There are only three basic precepts, and this one is perhaps the most basic of all. It directly underlies everything else the Temple does or teaches, and they interpret it more literally than any human religion I can remember. Listen. You can think of the Supreme Presence as a spiritual force pervading, shaping, organizing, guiding the entire universe. Its exact nature is such a subtle thing that it can *never* be put adequately into words. That's why, as I told you yesterday, Templemen spend lives of study trying to develop their intuitive grasp of it.

"What do they study? Anything and everything. Everything that exists or happens reflects the workings of the Supreme Presence. The more examples you know, the closer you can come to appreciating the extent and workings of the Way. But the emphasis in all this study is on observing and recording and appreciating—*never* on critical evaluation. On our way out of the monastery today, Chet and I had a chance to look at some of the relics on display there—souvenirs of the most extravagant miracles. Many of them were only witnessed by one Templeman, but in the eyes of the Temple they're no less respectable for that. And there's never any attempt at systematic analysis—because any attempt to describe things in terms of limited categories or simple relationships contradicts the 'infinitely varied' character attributed to the Supreme Presence. So it's irreverent at best, downright blasphemous at worst. So you can see how popular Terek is. What he's trying to do is well along toward the blasphemous end of the scale."

Kel looked slightly dazed. "I get the idea, more or less. But I'm still confused. If I understand you rightly—how can they believe that and get even as far as they have?"

"Very simple: they *don't* believe it—lock, stock, and barrel, to their deepest levels. They can believe intellectually and scholasticize *ad nauseam* about theological arguments like that—and all the while have enough intuitive understanding of natural law in their very bones to be able to walk across a room without killing themselves, no matter what they *say* they believe. And they *have* to have that kind of understanding, or they wouldn't have survived this far. They can even have enough to be able to build cannons that work some of the time. But their conscious, professed beliefs can keep them from learning to do any more than that. That's why it's so important to their future history to get Terek's concepts accepted here and now, while they have a chance."

"But," Kel protested, "*do* they have a chance? Did they ever have a chance? You're assuming we have to do something because we've ruined their chance. But from the way you describe the Temple's attitude, I don't see how they could have been accepted even if we'd never come here."

Still hoping it'll go away, Chet thought, this time with more conviction. "That," he said, "is because you're overlooking the rest of the picture. In untroubled times, you'd be right. Terek would be an unqualified boat-rocker with no redeeming social value and the dixar would have no patience with him. But as it is, the Temple has mixed feelings that let Terek get his foot in the door. They don't *like* the idea of accepting his notions—but they're pragmatic enough to be able to realize that maybe they'd better. The Ketaxil are threatening the very survival of the culture, and Kangyr knows it. And he can see that Terek's laws hold up well enough in demonstrations so that when Terek says he can give them the edge they need, he may be right. When we showed up, he wasn't quite ready to admit that openly, even to himself. But things that both he and Terek said lead me to think he was weakening. Without us, I'd guess Terek's laws would have been accepted and put to work within his lifetime. But we blundered in in Kangyr's moment of indecision and nudged him the wrong way. Some of our quasimaterials so obviously defy Terek's laws that Kangyr can jump on them as absolute disproof—thereby soothing the half of his conscience that wants to reject Terek. And killing Terek's chances."

He laughed sourly. "We thought quasimaterials were such a timely development—not only for our own use, but just what the doctor ordered for Yngmor's little communication setback. Well, it looks like we've come at just the right time to nip their science in the bud—by showing them just the wrong piece of advanced technology!"

Tina and Jem waited uncomfortably to see if he was going to say more. Even Kel was silent for several seconds. Then he cleared his throat and asked, "But is it really all that important? Sure, it is for Terek. But our concern has to be with the long-term welfare of the whole civilization, not one individual. If his work doesn't catch on now . . . well, somebody else will think of it later."

"Probably," Chet granted. "but who knows when? There are some times in history, Agent Kel, when an individual mind *is* of great importance. Try to picture just what's at stake here—from the standpoint of this culture, not ours. Just because Newton's laws—Terek's laws?—are now taught in the first week of every kid's science course, we think they're trivial. It's very hard for a modern person to do, but try to appreciate what a tremendous accomplishment it was to formulate them from scratch, when nobody knew them. It's a huge step which *can* happen when a certain point is reached—but it *doesn't* until some individual comes along capable of taking it. It still doesn't, unless the right things happen to suggest it and encourage him to follow through. That may take centuries.

"If Terek's done it and we let him be stopped, it may be centuries before it happens again. And a tremendous amount of the subsequent development of science and technology depends directly on that." He pulled one of the little quasimaterial balls out of his pocket and stared at it. "What we may have done to their history is absolutely appalling. Who would have thought that a little toy like this could wreck a culture?"

There was another awkward pause. It lasted a long time; this time even Kel didn't speak. Finally Tina asked softly, "What can we do about it?"

"I don't see that we can do anything." Kel interjected. "The damage is done, if it really is the damage you think it is. They've seen and touched quasimaterials, and we can't undo that. Maybe it'll even turn out better this way. Look—"

"I think," Chet interrupted bluntly, "you're just looking for the easiest way out for yourself, without thinking about the consequences. Maybe you can kid yourself that everything will turn out lovely if we just run away from the mess we've made, but I can't. Look, Kel, you do a lot of talking to remind us you have the ultimate say on what we do. Remember that maybe that means you get the responsibility for the consequences, too. If I can convince the bureau that your decision was directly to blame for a cultural disaster here, is that going to be good for you or anybody else?"

Kel stiffened and stared at him. "Are you threatening me?"

"I'm just asking a question. It's up to you to think about the answer. But don't expect me to tell any lies for you when we get home. Do you remember why we came? To help Yngmor survive. That's all. We didn't know it then, but apparently Terek was trying to help, too. I'm not sure exactly how, but I can make some guesses. Very likely, if Yngmor survived at all, it was going to be because of him. We may still be able to contribute something, but if we could be sure he had a fighting chance, I think the best thing we could do right now would be to get out of his way and leave. But we've got to get out of his way first. And I don't see how to do it."

"How about damping?" Jem said suddenly. "Maybe they'd—"

"Forget?" Chet's face brightened at the suggestion; then, just as quickly, he frowned and shook his head. "It's an idea, which is more than I had on my own. Thanks, Jem. But I don't think it's as good as we need. Yes, we could remote-trigger all the quasimaterials on the planet so nothing was left except the memory. But that would still be there. We could hope the natives would forget, but there's no guarantee that they would. And there's no guarantee that Terek will still be in the humor to push this when the climate improves. I think we'll have to write that approach off as too uncertain. Anybody have a better one?"

He looked at each of the others' faces in turn. Tina and Jem just shook their heads slowly. Kel seemed to be trying to glare at him and simultaneously avoid his gaze.

"Then," Chet said firmly, standing up with an air of dismissal, "we're going to have to just sit right here and wait until we think of one—preferably one that avoids that trouble. And soon—because they still need the help we came to give, and they need it soon." He started briskly back toward his cabin; there were things he needed to look up.

"Just a minute, Barlin."

The voice was Kel's. Chet stopped and turned back to look at him. "Yes, Agent Kel?"

Kel had been starting to light a new cigarette, but had stopped. The cigarette was still in his mouth, unlit; his hand that held the lighter seemed to be shaking slightly. "Just what," he demanded, "do you mean by 'they need it soon'?"

Chet looked and deliberated for a split second before he made his decision to spill it. Then he said matter-of-factly, "There's a wolf at the door. I talked to Ben Jonz this morning, and he thinks he sees a Ketaxil party heading this way. Yldac could be attacked again within a few days. So you see, the need for help against the barbarians is getting urgent—just when the cure we had in mind is beginning to look even worse than the disease."

12

Five fingers, Kangyr thought after the magicians left. *I never met a man with only five fingers before.* The thought lingered long after the magicians were gone—that thought and a feeling of almost-shame at the moment of weakness he had had as they left his chamber. It was far from fitting for a dixar to suggest the vulnerability of his own district to that extent. And yet, if it led to help in the form of magic comparable to that which had refuted Terek. . . .

Maybe it would be worth it.

Such thoughts led his mind back to the subject of Terek, down there on the wall—a subject which had occupied him far too much of late. Why did it have to be so mixed up? Why were there no clear answers?

Over and over during the day he found himself staring at the icon over the door of his chamber and turning matter over in his mind. Terek . . . the Ketaxil . . . the outlander magicians and their five fingers and strange magic which in truth surpassed anything even Kangyr had seen . . .

He was old. He had just admitted that to himself some time within the last few days. He couldn't even pinpoint the exact moment at which he did admit it, but he knew that what had brought it on had been his growing awareness of what he was up against.

And the fact that at some time—he couldn't say when, but perhaps not so terribly far off—he would have to Pass the Power. And along with it, very probably, the problems.

There was only one basic problem, of course. Survival. The Ketaxil. The problem was momentarily invisible right here, but he knew better than to assume that it was gone or even getting any better. Quite the contrary, in fact. Yldac itself had been struck often enough—and enough reports still managed to get here with the few boats which managed to survive this far en route from another Kengmor town—to keep him well aware that the menace was growing steadily worse. So he was doing all he could—things like resurrecting old cannons and training crews to man them. But the last attack, late this summer, was still fresh in his memory, and it hinted strongly that something more was needed.

But what? And to whom would he Pass the Power if the problem was still unsolved?

Shortly after Ravilyr had brought Terek's work to his attention. Kangyr had begun inquiring discreetly among the other Templemen with Disciples. He had hoped to find possible answers to both questions. Disappointingly, his inquiries about both kept leading him back to Terek. Of all the Disciples on hand, Terek was generally conceded to be the closest to a true Fledgling—in all respects but one.

But that one was a dilly. He was the only Disciple who was loudly and insistently preaching a clear and appalling heresy.

And, still more maddeningly, that heresy itself had seemed for a while the only thing that was likely to turn the tide against the Ketaxil.

How could such things be? Should not a Fledgling be clearly and unequivocally the stuff of which dixarl are made, and free of such glaring imperfections?

With an effort, Kangyr cast his mind far back, seeking to remember his own Fledgling days. And he saw that there had indeed been youthful indiscretions. Nothing as indiscreet as this, of course, but things which made him sure that he had not always had the ultimate wisdom. That had come only with the Power. Even after that, in fact, he could recall strange, disquieting nights during the first few years when he woke up alone in the darkness, plagued by doubts.

So perhaps there was hope for Terek. If only he could be made to see the utter folly of this one delusion he still clung to. But that was not as easy at it sounded. Not only was Terek stubborn, but there was always that Ketaxil thing looming over every decision. As long as it had seemed that Terek's so-called rules might provide the only way out, the difficulty had seemed almost insuperable. The rules were wrong, of course—but the wrong was so subtle that it seemed to defy all efforts to put it into words. How to admit that some of what Terek could seemingly do might be of great value to the Temple, without seeming at the same time to condone his heresy? How could he be made to see that, even if the Supreme Presence did choose to let him predict the motion of cannonballs with some semblance of accuracy for a while, it did not prove that those were the *only* ways things could be?

Now it seemed that these foreign magicians might have the answer. Even Terek could not continue indefinitely to deny the evidence of his eyes. No doubt his claiming to do so even this long was only the foolish pride of unrefined youth. But he would come around. He had to. Those things the magicians had were real, so simple that no trickery could be hidden in them, and they flatly contradicted Terek's claims. That fact would assert itself, louder and louder, until even Terek could no longer pretend to ignore it.

And if the magicians could also provide other kinds of help, perhaps there would be no need for the Temple to even consider giving any acceptance at all, however qualified and reluctant, to Terek's notions. They could be laid to rest with the unruffled, indifferent firmness they deserved.

Forever.

The thoughts stirred in Kangyr's mind all day, and gradually a kind of inner peace began to emerge. At Day's End he went down personally to take Terek off the wall. It was unusual—he saw a few awkwardly averted eyes as he walked slowly, alone and pensive, through the corridors—but it felt right. And no one could question it, whatever they might think.

When he stepped out into the courtyard, he was bathed at once in sensations which had rarely reached him for decades. A soft breeze caressed his face; the warmth the cobblestones had stored during the day filtered through the thin soles of his ancient sandals. The sky shaded delicately from almost black overhead, around the brooding towers where he lived, to a pale, luminous blue over the western wall.

It's beautiful, he thought suddenly. *I should come out more often.*

He found a solitary figure atop the wall, stark against the sky, standing motionless and looking toward the west. And he found the stairs that led up there.

He started up, taking his time and steadying himself against the wall. The stairs shook with his steps and he was not as sure of foot or as long of wind as he had once been. He had not yet thought about how he would get back up to his chamber. But he made it up the wall, and he felt an odd exhilaration as he stepped out onto the top and looked out over his town, with flickering lights beginning to appear in some of the windows. He couldn't quite remember when he had last seen it so close. . . .

Terek turned at the sound of his steps. His surprise was obvious, but beyond that his expression was impossible to read through the paint. "Dixar!" he said.

"Hello, Terek," Kangyr said quietly. "I've come to take you down." The vestment boxes and jars were still stacked around him; Kangyr opened one of the boxes and took out a metal key. Silently, he freed Terek's wrists, then bent down to take the shackles from his ankles. "There, " he said, standing again and laying the key aside. "Just one more thing. . . ."

He reached up. The helmet was incredibly heavy. He almost dropped it as he took it down and returned it to its box. "Your clothes are in one of the boxes," he reminded. "And there's water in one of the jars to wash the paint off."

Terek said nothing. Kangyr watched him as he stripped off the vestments and daubed away the paints, except for a few stubborn traces. As his own face came back into view, it seemed to Kangyr that his expression was oddly tranquil. He wished he could see what thoughts lay behind it. . . .

Terek finished putting on the tatters of his own clothes and glanced uncertainly at the boxes and jars. "Leave them," said Kangyr. "They will be attended to."

They started down the stairs together, the dixar at the heretical Disciple's side. "I hope," he said, "that these days have been profitable ones for you. Having seen your error, are you ready to return to the Truth?"

Terek grinned impudently. "I'm not convinced I was wrong, but I won't be preaching anymore for a while. But I think one of these days you'll see that you need at least some of what I offered you. And when you do, it's still available."

Kangyr shook his head sadly. "Such arrogance! But time will cure that." They reached the bottom of the stairs and turned, following the base of the wall. Kangyr's voice dropped, became confidential. "Terek, what do you know about those outlanders? I believe you were the first to notice their hands."

They reached one of the breezeways that opened onto Wall Street and stopped. A guard, his back toward them, stood stiffly at the other end, silhouetted against the brighter scene beyond. "I know nothing about them," Terek said, "but I suspect there's a lot I'd like to know." He grinned again. "Dixar," he said, gently chiding, "you're not getting ideas about using their parlor tricks instead of my new gunnery methods, are you?"

Kangyr looked away. That was exactly what he had in mind, although he didn't feel completely comfortable about it. From a theological viewpoint, he found the idea of dealing with the foreign magicians less disconcerting than dealing with Terek—at least they didn't try to clamp a tight harness of rules onto the Supreme Presence. Yet there was something which he couldn't quite place which bothered him about them, too. . . .

"Because if you are," Terek finished, "I think you'll find you have the same objections to them that you do to me. Good night, Dixar."

Terek strolled out the breezeway and off into the dusk toward his shack in the periphery, leaving Kangyr to puzzle over what his last remark meant.

As soon as Terek was out of the monastery and across Wall Street, his pace quickened and his expression and thoughts turned grimly introspective. As Kangyr had intended, he had had plenty of time to think on the wall, but the directions his thoughts had taken were not the ones Kangyr had hoped for. He had thought about his work, and his difficulties in getting it accepted. He had thought about the outlander magicians—where were they from, how were their tricks done, and what had happened when they were up there with Kangyr? He had seen them come out, and he had tried to call them to him again. They had heard him; he knew that. They had paused in the middle of Wall Street and stood there looking at him, hesitating as if uncertain whether to come. Then they had turned and hurried resolutely off without speaking—for which he could hardly blame them.

The question was still very much in his mind when Kangyr came down, and Terek had toyed with the idea of asking *him* exactly what had transpired. But he rejected that quickly. He had realized quite recently that there were other, safer ways to get such information if he really needed it. Meanwhile there was no need to advertise the fact that he had also finally found time to really examine his most fundamental attitudes toward the Temple itself—and they had emerged transformed.

For the moment, there were matters still more urgently demanding his immediate attention. He should have been home more than a day ago. How had Dajhek and Tolimra fared in his absence—and what did they know of where he had been?

His anger freshly stirred, he hurried through the narrow streets, occasionally taking a slight detour to avoid some shadowy figure he saw approaching. The streets were nearly deserted at this hour, and it was just as well to doubt the motives of anybody still afoot in them. Some such stragglers might well be harmless, or even friends, but if not it would be too late by the time he got close enough to be sure in this light. Already the blue-black dome above the rooftops was liberally sprinkled with stars, and the few lights slipping through shack windows merely reduced his dark adaptation without illuminating the streets.

The darkness was essentially complete by the time he rounded a corner and saw reflected stars dancing below the horizon and beyond the shore. Then it was just a few more steps to his own shack.

The door was open, and as he came to it a figure standing in the front turned and started to go inside, pulling it shut. "Tolimra!" Terek called out.

The figure flung the door wide open and whirled to face him. "Terek! Terek, is that you?"

Terek ran the last few steps. He placed his hands on her shoulders and leaned close enough so he could see her squinting to recognize him. "It is," she said finally. "We were worried about you, Terek. Where have you been? Here, come inside so I can see you and we can talk." She tugged at his arm to urge him inside ahead of her. Then she followed, pulling the door securely shut and saying toward the sleeping platform, "Terek's home, Dajhek."

Dajhek stirred slightly and mumbled something not quite coherent, then lay still again. The response was all Terek had really hoped for; Dajhek had not been having good days lately. At least he wasn't wheezing.

There were glowing coals in the fireplace and a tantalizing aroma of food superimposed on the old ingrained smells of the shack. By the glow of the wall fungi and the icon in the corner, Terek saw a kettle on the eating table and ventured to hope that his first worry had not been realized. "You've eaten?" he said.

Tolimra nodded, staring at his face and clothes. "Yes. Not last night; we waited and waited. By the time we got really worried it was too late to do anything else. But this morning. I can't go to market myself anymore, of course. But we have kindly neighbors, Terek. Kolamri, from across the way, brought us some tyraxet. And you, Terek. Have you eaten?"

"No." He almost laughed aloud at the way the question

took him by surprise. He'd been so busy thinking about his parents' problems and the other things that he hadn't even consciously thought about how hungry he was. Even though . . . "I haven't eaten since yesterday morning."

"That's terrible!" Tolimra gasped. "We shouldn't just be standing here talking. Here, we have some left . . ." She moved with surprising swiftness to get some tyraxet mush scraped from the kettle and into a bowl for Terek.

He had never before actually realized just how good such stuff could taste. As he wolfed it down, Tolimra sat silently for a while, watching him as if waiting for him to get his strength back before continuing the conversation. Finally she observed, "Your clothes are torn. What happened to you, Terek?"

He winced. "Haven't you heard anything?"

She didn't answer right away. Then she said, "I'd rather hear it from you."

He also waited, chewing his last mouthful twice as thoroughly as it needed before he finally swallowed it and spoke. "I was on the wall," he said. "As a Dunce."

"Oh, no!" Tolimra whispered, chagrined. "I heard the rumor. But the neighbors didn't want to talk about it. And I didn't want to believe it."

"Well, it's true."

"But, surely . . . there must be some mistake."

"No," said Terek. "There's no mistake."

"There *must* be. Some overeager young Templeman trying to curry favor—"

"No," Terek interrupted, looking straight at her. "He put me there himself." He nodded at the glowing icon of Kangyr.

Tolimra stared at him for a long time, barely beginning to believe, nowhere close to understanding. Finally she asked quietly, "How did it happen?"

The mental suffering it caused her was painful to see. Terek's own had ended on the wall. "You knew I was doing some work with some of the writings that were brought back from Ybhal."

"Yes."

"There were some ideas there that seemed worth following up. I did, and they got me into the trouble—they and some foreign magicians. It would take too long to tell you just what the ideas were, but one of them concerns some patterns of behavior that moving bodies seem to follow. The other is that Ymrek itself is just a falling body, moving around the Day Star."

"But the Day Star moves around—"

"No, it doesn't. They've always taught us that, but it's just a different way of looking at things. My way's simpler. I tried to make them see that, but the idea seemed to scare them. So did the other one. For a while we—Ravi and I—thought they were going to find a way to work that one into their scheme because it might help us ward off the Ketaxil. But the dixar never liked the idea because he thought it violated the First Precept."

He stopped. Tolimra waited expectantly, then said, "You mentioned a magic show. What do they have to do with it?"

"They had some good tricks—some things which seemed to violate my patterns. The dixar took them as proof that I was wrong and put me up as a Dunce. I guess he thought it would cure me."

Tolimra stared at him as if afraid to ask exactly what he meant by that. Instead she asked, "Why didn't you just admit you were wrong and spare yourself and all of us this humiliation?"

"Because I'm *not!*" He stopped, startled. He couldn't remember raising his voice in anger at Tolimra before. "I'm not wrong," he repeated, more quietly but no less stubbornly. "And because I'm not wrong, I wasn't humiliated. I refused to be."

Tolimra's whole face drooped. He could hardly hear her as she said slowly, "Then you really are a heretic? My offspring . . . a heretic?"

"Yes," he said, almost fiercely. "The worst kind. I finally admitted it to myself when I was out there on the wall all night and all day. Kangyr wanted me to have time to think. Well, I had it, and this is what it did for me. Before that I'd kept telling myself that I still really believed in the Temple's teachings and it was just a matter of looking at things the right way to fit my ideas into theirs. But today I gave it up. If the dixar himself keeps telling me that the Temple and I contradict each other, who am I to contradict him on *that* point? So I finally came right out and admitted that my ideas and the Temple teachings *aren't* compatible . . . and I still say mine are right."

"Terek!"

"My rules of motion reject the First Precept. Ymrek's motion rejects the Covenant from Before Time. There's only one thing left I hadn't get around to rejecting, at least out loud, and I took care of that one a few hours ago. So now I've sunk as low as I can get—and I feel like I've just been released from prison."

Tolimra was crying now, in the tearless, spasmodically sobbing way of Kemrekl. "I don't understand," she said over and over. "I don't understand. How could you do this?" She stared at him silently for a long time, breathing slowly and heavily. Then she said, "This last thing you say you rejected. Surely you can't mean. . . ."

Her voice trailed off. She couldn't bring herself to say it. "There's only one thing I can mean," Terek said harshly. "The dixar is just a man." Tolimra began sobbing uncontrollably. He reached over and patted her gently; she seemed to ignore the gesture. "I'm sorry, Tolimra," he said softly. "But that's the only way I can make sense out of it all. "I'm sorry for him, too. He's a man, honestly well-meaning but utterly misguided through very little fault of his own. He's trapped in a system that he inherited and they've told him what he is for so long that he's started believing it." He looked over at the softly glowing icon and visualized the reality it was supposed to represent, trudging up the stairs to take his chains off. "Now that I realize that, I feel a lot more charitable toward him than I've been doing lately. It's not all his fault. Nobody should have to think of himself that way."

Tolimra sobbed a good while longer without looking at him. When she did finally look up, she seemed exhausted. "I still don't understand," she said weakly. "But I guess I can believe it's happened. So now what, Terek? Are you going back to the monastery?"

He nodded. "Of course," he said quietly. "I have to, for two reasons. I can't tell them what I've told you; I'd end up in an execution pit. So I'll go on as I have been, as far as they're concerned. I know what I believe now; they don't have to."

"What if I tell them? Tolimra asked suddenly.

"Will you?"

"No," she sighed, after trying to hold the bluff for a few seconds. "But I am shocked. And I feel almost as guilty about covering for you as I would about reporting you."

"I understand," Terek nodded. And he did.

"How is Ravilyr going to take this?" she asked abruptly. "He was so proud of you."

"For all I know," said Terek, with a mixture of uncertainty and tentative bitterness, "he still is. I haven't seen Ravi since I was sentenced. But I know I have to keep pushing my ideas because Yngmor needs them. That's the other reason I have to go back to the monastery."

"Someday," Tolimra said doubtfully, "maybe I'll admire you for this. Meanwhile . . . what about those outlanders?"

"I don't know," said Terek, suddenly tight-lipped. "But I'm not going to let them stop me. You can count on that."

13

It had been a taxing day, and Chet felt a wave of relief sweep over him as Tina turned the lights down, crawled under the covers, and stretched out next to him in the darkness. He lay there for several minutes, waiting for sleep, then noticed that his eyes weren't even shut. Annoyed, he shifted slightly and resolved to concentrate on a methodical relaxation routine.

But as he moved, Tina lightly laid her hand on his under the blanket and said quietly, "I don't expect much sleep either. Not with that hanging over me."

Chet let his fingers curl around hers and he postponed his relaxation ritual. "Quite a situation, isn't it?"

"That's putting it mildly. Chet, do you think we'll find a way to fix it?"

"I really hope so. I would say we must . . . but right now I'm not confident enough that we will to put any money on it." He waited a few seconds, then added bitterly, "I don't think we'd better count on any help from Kel."

"That's putting it mildly, too. I almost think what he'd like more than anything else is just to hightail it away from here and pretend we never saw this."

"He would," said Chet. "I'm practically sure of it."

"What?"

"Of course. He practically said it in so many words. Oh, he made it sound like his reason was simply that he honestly didn't believe anything was seriously wrong here. That's probably even partly true, or at least it was at the beginning of our little chat this afternoon. He's given us ample evidence that he doesn't really understand anything about this planet, and I don't think it even particularly bothers him. I don't think any of us has any delusion that he's too bright. But under all that, I think there's something even more important. He's afraid that if we do stay and look into it, we'll find out that something is very definitely very wrong. And we'll not only have to try to fix it, but we'll have to report both our blunder and our attempts to salvage it. Which just might also be blunders."

"But what else is there to do? If we have done what we think we have, we can't just let the mess stay that way. I can't see anything else we can do but try to fix it."

"Kel can. You don't think he really cares about these people, do you?" Chet grimaced. "All he cares about is Bydron Kel. He's a career bureaucrat, Tina, and not much more than that. He's low enough on the totem pole to care very much about rising higher and gaining security, and he's been at it just long enough to learn that doing a good job isn't always the best way to do that. Try to see it his way—for just a minute or so; I like you a lot better than him. Here he is in sole command of a pretty responsible position that seemed routine until this happened. Now he has to actually think about a hard problem—if we admit there really is a hard problem—and he may make a wrong decision and Flangan will know it. But if we don't follow it up, there's an excellent chance nobody on Larneg will ever know what he did. Because if we let it alone, the important consequence will be a nonhappening. Even if a follow-up party comes out here later, they'll never suspect anybody like Terek existed. That would suit Kel just fine."

"But *we* have consciences to live with," Tina said bitterly.

"Yes. It's really something, when you think about it. Look back through history and you find it liberally sprinkled with power-hungry men who wanted to rule whatever world they happened to live on. Very few of them ever got the chance. Now we've progressed to the point where a character like Kel gets it handed to him, just to keep him out of people's hair back on Larneg. Not his *own* world, of course. But somebody's."

"Of course. Chet, I've been trying to figure out what he

does have up his sleeve. Do you think he has his mind made up in advance to veto Project Airfloat no matter what?"

"I think he's pretty determined. But I don't think his mind has much to do with it. I have a hunch he's under strict orders to act as a rubber stamp for Flangan."

"I get that impression, too. But I'm still puzzled. I've been trying to fit it all together so it makes sense, but I don't quite see it. What's Flangan's angle?"

"He's a career bureaucrat, too. A much older one than Kel, with enough experience to know all the tricks. And enough of that security Kel's working for to be very wary of boat-rockers. He knows he's in an agency which hasn't really done anything important for years. But it's given him a cozy niche that he'll be delighted to keep until he retires or dies. And he knows that that depends on keeping the purse-string holders convinced that it's worthwhile to keep supporting alien culture studies. But only the most thoroughly innocuous culture studies. Anything else and somebody might start looking too close and begin to think the BEL has outlived its usefulness. You'll notice he hasn't approved anything else. Not that I've heard about, anyway."

"Nor I." Tina giggled—a characteristic sound of pure little-girlish amusement with which she occasionally startled some of her more staid colleagues, now suffused with a cynically derisive note. "You know, it just occurred to me that we might be the first real boat-rockers he's had to deal with. How many others do you suppose have actually gone back to Larneg from a field site to make a personal request for permission to intervene?"

"I've never heard of one," said Chet. He had never thought of that before, but it was true. "I guess we really rattled him. But that doesn't change my guesses about what went through his mind before he decided to approve our request. It makes them seem ever solider. He would have liked to just turn us down and declare Ymrek a closed case; there's no real doubt about that. But I think he was afraid, after talking to us. Afraid that we'd raise a public stink that might hurt him even more than letting us go back thinking we might get to do what we wanted. Especially If we went back with a nice tame field agent to baby-sit us and make sure we didn't get out of hand."

"You mean," said Tina, and Chet mentally saw her eyes widen in the darkness, "you think he actually sent us back here with no intention at all of letting us carry out our mission? Just for his own security?"

"I do indeed. Oh, it's possible that he's hoping to get some minor observational data out of our preliminary studies—something harmless but maybe good for publicity. Maybe something for this fellow who's trying to develop a sociological perturbation theory, for instance. But at best, anything like that is incidental. The main thing is for Kel to find something in our preliminary results to use as an excuse to keep us from doing any more—hopefully a good enough excuse to keep us quiet and docile."

"He underestimates us," Tina said darkly. "You know, Chet, sometimes I think I understand aliens better than people."

"That's why you're a xenologist," he told her, laughing slightly and reaching around to give her far shoulder a playful squeeze. "I know *one* people you understand just fine. But"—his voice became a shade more serious—"I understand why you think that. You see more of our oddities because you're standing too close to us."

"Or not close enough to them." There was no hint of giggle in her voice now. "I wake up thinking about that sometimes. We so seldom really see them as individuals. Even right here among them, we're so detached we tend to think about them in sweeping abstractions about cultures and tribes and historical turning points. But that's not the reality that ultimately matters. Any society or history is made up of individuals. Terek's the first one here we've even begun to see that way—and I've seen just enough of how things might look to him to scare me." They were both silent for some time. Then Tina said slowly, "You know what I think scares me most?"

"What?"

"The thought that we may wind up going to Larneg and having to look Flangan in the eye and tell him he was right.

About what he said when he told us we could come back here."

Chet stared into the blackness, thinking about that. Neither of them said any more. He could tell from the sound and feel of her breathing that Tina went to sleep first.

For him, sleep was slow in coming, and fitful when it came. . . .

There were dreams. Many dreams, Chet knew—too many. But only one that survived.

A distant part of his mind tried to tell him it was a dream. But once, at least, it had been real. . . .

He was on a spaceship, one which he would later call tiny—the shuttle from Larneg to the permanent industrial space stations. But it wasn't tiny in those days, for Chet himself was only four years old, and not large for his age.

He had never been in space before, but he had heard enough to be sure he wanted to go along when he heard his Uncle Nelz talking about riding out to the station with a friend who was going to work there. Chet didn't like the friend—a big, round, noisy man name Mr. Nordzik, in baggy brown overalls—but Nelz was his favorite uncle. Nelz, laughing and talking easily while bouncing Chet on one knee, had even talked his mother out of the few reservations she had about letting Chet go.

Now they were here and Chet was wide-eyed every minute of the trip, busily absorbing all the new sensations. He stayed quite close to Nelz, of course—while the new sensations were fascinating, their unfamiliarity made it hard to be completely at ease with them. The takeoff had actually been a little scary, with the noise and the pressure on his body, but that had soon stopped and left him unharmed. In the stillness that followed, he felt very light-headed, then light all over—almost as if he could float through the air, but not quite. That had been a little scary, too, at first, but not like the takeoff. And it had already lasted so long, without changing, that Chet had about decided it was harmless, and even fun. It felt a little like drifting off to sleep.

Finally he felt so much at ease that he actually left Nelz's side and took to running around the single big cabin, exploring. There was so much to see. There were pipes and gauges all over, way up by the ceiling. There were even more of them up in the front, in the glass cage where two silent men in blue uniforms sat on high brown padded stools with their backs to the cabin. Nelz said they were driving the shuttle. Big black boxes, strapped down with wide yellow bands, took up most of the floor space. Chet spent many happy minutes pounding on them and trying to guess what was inside.

He looked at the viewscreens in the glass cage, slanted out just below the ceiling so the drivers had to look up to see them. Chet looked up, too, but quickly lost interest in them. They were just television pictures, and in them he couldn't even see their motion through the stars. But the two small ports he found aft were another matter. Those were actual ports—round windows—and even though he couldn't see their motion through them either, he could press his nose against the cold glass and shake his eyes and look out and know that he was looking directly into space itself. That was Larneg back there, and those were the stars. Nelz said that they were suns, like Capella, and many of them had whole other worlds like Larneg.

Chet was staring out, trying to picture that—to *really* picture it—when the horrible scream rang out behind him. Shocked, he whirled away from the port to see what was wrong.

There were only a couple of other passengers besides himself and Nelz and Mr. Nordzik. One of them, a thin pale man with curly hair, had screamed; he was still making gagging noises as he reeled and staggered along the pile of boxes, one hand at his throat and the other clutching a dark green bottle. The bald man he had been sitting next to got up and slapped him on the back and said something like, "What's the matter, fella? Go down the wrong way?"

Then Mr. Nordzik was on his feet, staring wide-eyed. He came lurching through the aisle, clumsy in the weak pseudograv, and knocked the bald man away from the other. The bald man hurtled backward and landed in a heap across the arm of his chair. "What's the matter with you?" he bellowed. "Can't you see—"

"I can see," Mr. Nordzik bellowed back. "This man's poisoned! Nelz—"

Nelz was already on his feet, half running forward. The bald man gasped, slapped the back of his hand across his own mouth, and stared as Mr. Nordzik got the poisoned man in a wrestling hold and pried the bottle out of his hand. Nelz was up front, pounding on the glass and yelling, "Medic!" The drivers didn't seem to hear, at first. Then Nelz noticed a red telephone on one wall and yelled the same thing into it. Both drivers looked around, startled. One of them jumped up, threw open an invisible door, and came running out into the cabin.

"What's the trouble?" he barked. Then he saw Mr. Nordzik and the thin man with the curly hair, and the bottle. "Oh . . . " he said weakly, and he and Nelz hurried back to help Mr. Nordzik. They grabbed the poisoned man's arms and legs and tried to hold him still. "What was he doing with that, anyway?" the uniformed driver muttered. "Any fool'd know better than to drink—"

"He thought it was something else," the bald man snapped from his chair. "Can't you quit talking and do—"

"What is it, Captain?" Nelz asked, ignoring the bald man and squinting at the green bottle. "I don't recognize—

"—," said the captain. It was a long word that meant nothing to Chet. "Lethal. Not slow."

"Do you have an antidote on board?"

The captain shook his head grimly. "Not a drop. Never imagined we'd need one. Not for that." He looked puzzled. The poison victim had quit struggling and gone limp. He was so still that for a sickening instant Chet was afraid he was dead. Chet had never seen anybody dead before. . . .

Then the man twitched and a feeble sound came from his throat. Chet saw that with great relief. "Not much time," he heard someone mutter. The captain was staring at the green bottle. "Noncorrosive . . . tastes like hell. . . ."

Suddenly he grabbed up the bottle. "Hold his mouth

open," he snapped to Nelz and Mr. Nordzik. He moved the bottle toward the curly-haired man's face.

The bald man jumped out of his chair and lunged toward them. "Captain!" he yelled. "Are you crazy? You can't—"

"Siddown!" the captain thundered, staring fiercely and readying a leg to kick in a split second. The bald man reeled back uncertainly, shaking and staring at his friend.

Nelz said, "Are you sure you—"

"Never mind," the captain interrupted impatiently. "I'll do it myself." He braced the victim against the boxes, forced his head back and his mouth open, and poured the poison down his throat as fast as it would go. Some of it spilled out, dribbling down his cheek, but most of it went down, and when the captain dropped the bottle, it was empty.

There was a shocked hush for about five seconds. Then the victim's shoulders began to heave and he started making gasping noises, louder and faster. He exploded into a series of gagging sounds, kicked and broke free of the captain's grip. The captain make no attempt to get him back. The victim ran drunkenly around the boxes once, then dropped abruptly to his hands and knees, not far from Chet, and threw up, violently.

When he was finished, his gasps and heaves gradually subsided. Little Chet stared for a few seconds, then looked away. He was feeling a little nauseous himself. . . .

He heard the captain saying, "He'll be okay now. That stuff provokes vomiting itself, if you get a big enough swig of it. Not the nicest way to get it out, but it's all we had. With that out of his system, I know I can save him. . . ."

At that point the older Chet woke up, still breathing heavily from the vivid autobiographical nightmare. The images were still very close to the surface, but now he was here, in his and Tina's bed, in comforting quiet darkness, with Tina asleep at his side. . . .

And he had the answer.

He told the others about it in the morning, at breakfast. They were seated, as at most of their meals, in the only real chairs aboard the boat: the ones in the fore cabin. Each had a small folding tray with a depression molded to fit the ration tins served up by the galley, and though the arrangement lacked class, it was the closest to real dining facilities they could muster in the cramped quarters.

Because of his timing, Chet cut his story to a skeletal outline, skipping all the graphic details. Even so, Kel looked increasingly annoyed. When Chet finished, the BEL man stared at him and said, "So what? You had a dream. It's morbid. It's sick. Why bother us with it? And at breakfast, of all times?" Frowning irritably, he noisily folded his used ration tin up for recycling and got out a cigarette.

"I did it," Chet said evenly, "because we have a problem. And I think our problem is a lot like that."

Out of the corner of his eye, he saw Tina start to grin knowingly. Kel just kept frowning and said, "I fail to see the connection."

"The shuttle passenger with the poison was cured by giving him a massive overdose of the same poison. Right? Not always safe, but sometimes it works. It depends on the poison. I think our poison is one that can work that way."

"I still don't see what you're driving at."

"Simply this. Our blunder was showing them quasimaterials that seemed to violate Terek's laws. Well, I think the clergy must have some prejudices of their own about what's reasonable. Like Tina said yesterday, they couldn't even walk across a room safely if they didn't. So let's try to violate a few of those prejudices. Let's give them a *real* magic show, on a grand scale!"

Kel had been inhaling; he coughed suddenly. "You're crazy!" he gasped.

"For instance," said Chet, ignoring him, "I think some Reynolds airfloaters, introduced to the right people with the right degree of flamboyancy, might shake them up a bit. Kangyr, anyway. We're all set to produce them—they're what we came here for, remember? And the market's very ripe for them right now, considering what Ben said yesterday. If the Ketaxil really have the souped-up offense they're supposed to have, the Kengmorl could use some souped-up defense. We could give them a little of that when they need it, instead of afterward, and maybe solve our problem at the same time."

"Out of the question," Kel snapped. "A few little quasi-material trinkets are one thing and a full-scale floater is quite another—"

"Exactly," Chet nodded, smiling amiably.

"I gather you don't even plan to use any caution in working up to the floater—"

"None whatever," Chet agreed. "It would defeat the purpose. We want to see if Kangyr can be shocked. If he'd decide our floaters are so nutty he's rather deal with Terek, that would suit me fine."

"Highly unpredictable," Kel objected. "It's not in the range of our contingency plans. And the preliminary study isn't even complete."

"And it won't be! Can't you see yet that we've messed things up in a big way and we have to change our tack to try to fix them?"

"But," Kel spluttered, "you're talking about a large-scale cultural interference! Barlin, what are you trying to do to my career?"

Chet turned and stared at the BEL agent with frank disgust for several seconds. "I could care less about your career," he said finally, evenly, "but it wouldn't be easy. I care very much, though, about the fact that we have *already* committed a large-scale cultural interference and it's going to take a comparable one to fix it. We can't guarantee the cure, but we can't leave knowing we've messed things up this thoroughly and made no attempt at one. So, Agent Kel, about your career—you try to keep us from doing anything, when we get home I'll testify against you as strongly as I can."

"And so will I," said Tina.

"And I," said Stiv.

"And I," said Jem.

A trapped look began to creep over Kel's features. Chet told him quietly, "So you see where we stand. That's what's going to happen if we go back and have to tell them what happened and what you did about it. Think how you'll fare in that." He waited silently to see if Kel would say anything, then added, "If you have a better idea, we're desperately eager to hear it—and I'm not being sarcastic. But if you don't . . ."

He let his voice trail off, then looked purposefully away from Kel and started getting out his pipe and tobacco.

Nobody said anything for many seconds. Then Kel said tightly, "I don't have to decide right this minute. I'll have to think about it for a few hours, anyway. And if you go and do anything without my approval—you'll regret it." He stood up and stomped out of the cabin, heading for his stateroom.

Chet shrugged slightly and puffed methodically on his pipe, giving no other indication that he had heard.

The day passed slowly and quietly, with an undercurrent of tension that was almost entirely felt rather than voiced. None of the party went outside. They spoke seldom to each other—and never to Kel. And he said nothing to any of them. Most of the day he spent alone in his stateroom.

Chet reflected several times during the day that, in certain senses, he actually felt sorry for Kel. The man was out of his element—probably more so here than he had ever been before. He was one of the two members of the party who spent essentially all their time in the cramped quarters of the boat—and, unlike Stiv Sandor, a pilot by choice, he was not well suited to that. Nor was he well adapted to living comfortably and harmoniously in prolonged close proximity with four other people—especially four whose backgrounds and goals were completely different from his own. He was most definitely not up to making far-reaching decisions about huge, subtle, completely unprecedented problems.

He could probably function fairly comfortably—and harmlessly—in a routine desk job on Larneg, by the book. But this was no routine desk job, and it could not be done by the book. Here he was very much a victim of his own weaknesses of character.

But that, Chet reminded himself sternly, could in no way excuse the harm he could do.

In midafternoon, Chet gave Ben Jonz another call to ask about the Ketaxil he thought he'd seen. "They're still there," Ben said. "And still moving toward you."

"Prognosis?"

"Uncertain. I'll be surprised if they don't hit Yldac. But I'll also be surprised if they do it in less than a full day. They'd have to travel hard all night, and we've never seen them do anything like that yet."

Chet broke the connection without feeling especially encouraged. He felt more and more anxious to get away from here soon—and less and less hopeful of doing so. Even a full day wasn't much.

They all met in the fore cabin for supper—even Kel. But he stared stiffly straight ahead through the entire meal, and the others talked as if he weren't there.

Finally, when the others stood up to return their tins to the galley, he spoke. "Just a minute," he said very quietly. "I have something to say."

They all stopped and turned to look at him, but nobody said anything. Kel didn't look directly at any of them, but he said, in the same tone, "That plan of yours, Barlin. You have my consent. My most grudging consent."

And then, without waiting for reply or picking up his tin, he got up and walked briskly back to his stateroom. Chet waited until he heard the door close—softly, despite the obvious attempt at slamming—to react.

Then he turned Jem with a grin. "Okay, quasimaterial man—we're ready to go into production!"

And Jem grinned back. At last the sorcerer's apprentice would be the star of the show.

14

What all quasimaterials have in common is that they are artificial standing wave structures qualitatively similar to ordinary matter—although in general their actual energy content is much lower. And, just as computer-generated sounds can have properties "natural" sounds can't, or hologram images can be made of objects which could never "really" exist, they can have properties wildly unlike those of ordinary matter. Some, like the outer hull of the landing boat, are totally invisible from at least one direction. Some, like some of the trinkets Tina peddled after their exploratory magic shows—the balls Kangyr had shown them, for instance—have inequivalent gravitational and inertial masses. Most can be induced to damp out and vanish exponentially—like Instavac, or the ghost statues Chet used to finish the magic shows.

The special qualities of the Type 76CB3 control elements used in Reynolds airfloaters are a little harder to describe.

Chet and Tina watched with interest as Jem put the finishing touches on their first floater early the next morning. Mostly it consisted of real matter, a cheap, easily shaped synthetic that emerged ready-formed from an automatic fabricator. A casual observer would never have guessed that—the fabricator was programmed to imitate minutely skilled handcrafting of wood, even to the extent of providing different minor flaws in each unit.

To Chet, the effect was completely convincing, and he was necessarily seeing it at quite close range. The aft stowage was the only place in the boat big enough to make the floaters, to say nothing of having the only hatches big enough to get them out once they were finished. But it was not big enough to allow any extra space. As soon as Kel had given in last night, they had started rearranging things, packing boxes as tightly as possible against the stern wall and moving the cart and a good many other things to the forward cabin. That left room to set the fabricator up against one side wall, with space in front of it to deposit its finished product. Late at night they had watched it come out—first a shapeless blob of brown, then the clearly recognizable prow of a boat, moving slowly and smoothly forward until a complete small boat lay on the floor, stretching all the way from the fabricator's exit chute to the landing boat's far cargo hatch.

It had taken an hour. Now, lying there occupying almost all the cleared space, with Jem kneeling in the bow, it could easily have passed for the handiwork of some tribe of woodcraft-skilled barbarians in some far-distant region of Ymrek. Had they not known the truth, either Chet or Tina might have taken it for that with complete confidence. It would have taken sophisticated chemical analysis to prove it was anything else.

Even the control elements, which Jem was now installing, were made to resemble carved sticks mounted in crude swivels in the bottom of the boat. But Jem had to mount them by hand, and as he worked they often seemed to want to float, or occasionally jump, from his hands. The front one went in without much trouble; the one in back took a little longer. But finally the job was finished and Jem stood up with a look of satisfaction.

"Finished?" Tina asked.

"Almost. But I thought since we're planning to play this magic bit to the hilt, one little finishing touch might be in order." He reached into the pouch of quasimaterials he carried inside his magician's robe and produced something which he attached to the prow of the floater. "Like it?"

Chet looked at the figurehead for a few seconds, then quickly away. At first glance it was just a three-pronged fork, pointing forward. But just a little closer examination showed that it was one of those visual paradoxes that can be drawn in perspective (and had been, by artists at least as far back as Escher) but could never actually be built in three dimensions—with ordinary matter. The eye quickly became hopelessly confused as to what was prong and what was space.

It made Chet dizzy to look at it. "Perfect!" he laughed.

"Good," Jem chuckled smugly. "Then I guess we're ready to go." He climbed back over the gunwale and sat down, very low, in the bow. Tina and Chet followed, sitting behind him in single file.

"Ready?" Chet asked. They didn't want the hatch open any longer than necessary. . . .

Jem nodded. Chet called forward, and somewhere up in the fore cabin Stiv Sandor pushed a button. With an almost inaudible whirr, the big cargo hatch yawned open to bright clear morning before them. Jem took the front control element in his left hand and the long rod linked to the rear element in his right. He moved each level the merest trifle—

And the floater lifted inches off the deck and floated silently out through the hatch. As they cleared, Chet held onto the gunwales beside Tina and glanced back just in time to see the hatch shut after them, leaving the boat again invisible. Looking over the side, he saw the ground a few yards below, then falling away as Jem pulled back sharply on his front stick to be sure they would clear the highest parts of the barrier thicket. Tina grabbed Chet's hands tightly and asked, "How does it work, Jem?"

"You never rode one before?" Jem sounded surprised. "Gravity. The strength and direction of the force on each control element depends on its orientation relative to the gravitational field. It's a little like the way the force on an electron in a magnetic field depends on which way it's moving—but not very much. Anyway, I can make gravity move each end of the floater in any direction I like just by moving the control elements around. Like this." Without further warning, he suddenly made the floater twist wildly, stopping just short of pitching the crew overboard, then chuckled at Tina's reaction and settled back to a smooth but steep glide.

They barely cleared the nearest of the ash trees which rose above the tangled understory of the thicket. Of all the vegetation they had seen, the ash trees underwent the most striking seasonal changes, and no human had yet seen the whole cycle. By a few days ago the yellow-green of the leaves had been almost entirely replaced by mottled patterns of black and silver. Today the silver, too, had gone and the trees stood uniformly black, as if making a last-ditch effort to catch every possible photon before winter set in. But the effort was not entirely successful—this morning, from this angle, they glistened like millions of razor-thin obsidian knives in the early sunshine slanting across them.

Jem kept climbing as they crossed the barrier thicket, reaching a peak of over a thousand feet and starting downward only after they emerged over the open plain surrounding the town. As they went over the top the entire town came into view sprawled out before them.

The town—and the water around it.

"Look!" Tina gasped suddenly, pointing off the bow to the left. "What are those?"

Chet looked and didn't like what he saw on the water. "One, two, three . . . seven," he counted. "I guess Ben was wrong. Today's the day."

"Ketaxil?" Tina asked.

"I'd say so. Can't be sure without glasses, but they look right. Ben thought they wouldn't get here today because they'd have to travel all night. Look like they did." He thought silently for a few seconds, then mused, "I wonder what they really do have in the way of weapons? And what kind of defense improvements Terek was trying to peddle to the Temple."

"I doubt that they have antiaircraft guns," Jem said, looking curiously at the boats approaching Yldac. "Want to go over for a closer look?" He veered slightly to the left.

"No!" Tina said instantly. Jem unveered.

"Probably not a good idea, Jem," Chet said. "They might surprise you, and we're not exactly armed to the teeth." They weren't completely unarmed this trip—along with the other paraphernalia befitting powerful magicians from afar, each had allowed himself the luxury of a compact beamer, just in case. Effective, under the right conditions, but far from limitless in capability. Chet cast one more glance at the boats bobbing half-silhouetted among the dancing reflections not far to the northeast. "This might not be the best possible day for this, but the show must go on. Let's get down to that castle as quick as we can."

As they descended steeply toward the center of the town, a few people in the streets below looked up, saw them, and scattered into houses with considerable commotion. They were far enough below to appear antlike and insignificant, and Chet thought only in passing of the possible significance of being seen by them. Jem ignored them and headed the boat faster and faster down toward the castle at the summit of the monastery. They passed over Wall Street low enough to faintly hear a small burst of commotion below; Chet looked down to see a group in the marketplace scatter for shelter.

And he caught a glimpse of a single figure standing his ground and watching the sky without moving, right in the middle of the wide street, as the others fled.

By then they were on a level with the upper portions of the castle and still descending. The approach would have been terrifying in any conventional craft, and Jem was taking the floater in fast enough, and through enough turbulence, to keep the passengers from getting too smug. He was heading for a sort of protected balcony that might be considered part of the lowest level of the castle proper, a couple of levels above the gardened terrace with its prominent ash trees. Almost to the end the bleak vertical wall rushed straight toward them. Then, in the last few yards, Jem slowed them to a gentle landing on the balcony.

It felt almost snug. The shelf was not especially big, and was thoroughly concealed from any eyes below, with a thick black wall some six feet high running around the outer edge and several round towers and stacks rising like giant tree trunks around them. But there was a closed door in the inner wall here. . . .

"This must be the place," Jem said, "Now what? We probably shouldn't sit here too long without some plan."

"Have to get inside," Chet said. "I'm pretty sure the dixar's chamber is in the extreme top level—that little box right up there in the middle. But it doesn't seem to have any doors or windows on the outside."

"Sure doesn't. Seems odd, but I don't remember noticing any when they took us up there from inside. . . . Hm-m-m. Hang on." He lifted off again, lowered the floater over the edge, and ran it methodically along the wall below in search of an opening.

He found one at the first corner and hovered in front of it to size it up. It was nothing more than a plain rectangular window, a mere hole in the wall, not very big, with bare stone all the way to the edges, no glass or grate, and vacant blackness beyond. It looked out of the question. But a Reynolds airfloater, almost free of aerodynamic forces and drawing its power in a highly controllable way from the highly reliable gravitational field, has a maneuverability such as pilots of conventional craft seldom even dream about.

"Duck," Jem said finally. He eased the floater through the window, barely clearing the sides. Nothing happened; luckily the hall seemed to be empty. Others wouldn't, but by then they should be better able to react. There were torches, flickering and oily-smelling, on the walls; Jem hovered just inside the window to allow their eyes to adjust to the torchlight. Then he headed along the empty hall until he found a stairway. He tilted the floater's nose upward to match the slope of the stairs and started up, never touching, but occasionally maneuvering delicately past an almost impossibly tight turn.

The stairs rose three levels and then leveled off into a familiar short corridor. At the other end was a big wooden door—and a Templeman. When he saw them float out of the stairwell, he let out a gasp clearly audible the length of the hall and then stood frozen—except for some protective religious gestures which he managed to get through in great haste. Jem pulled the floater almost to within a lance length of him and halted.

Chet grinned broadly at the Templeman. “Good morning,” he said, his hand resting lightly on the beamer just inside his robe. “We’ve come to see Kangyr on business. You will please admit us—and I suggest you don’t attempt to raise your lance. Right where it is will be fine.”

Kangyr’s eyebrows rose quite noticeably when they floated through the open door—much more so than when he had counted their fingers. *“What,”* he demanded, staring at the bow of the floaters, “is *that?* “

“Your Holiness wondered if our magic could help you,” Chet said as Jem eased the floater along one side of the long table, “and I said I’d have to consult the spirits. This is their answer. And none too soon, I might add.”

Jem stopped the floater when the bow was just a few feet from Kangyr, holding it just high enough so the humans’ faces were on a level with the dixar’s. Kangyr, tight-lipped, swept his eyes quickly along its length, then looked sharply at Chet. “What do you mean by that?”

Before Chet could answer, the faint sound of an explosion, muffled by distance and the indirectness of its path, reached them. Kangyr’s expression changed abruptly. “The Ketaxil are back,” Chet said quietly.

Kangyr nodded solemnly, then seemed to turn fiercely defiant. “We’ve stood them off before!” he said hotly. “We can do it again, just as we’ve done in the past.” His gaze returned to the floater suspended three feet above the floor, full of what Chet was pretty sure was suspicion.

More guns boomed in the distance—more, it seemed to Chet, than he would have thought available, from what he had seen so far. He wished he could see what was going on out there. All that was certain was that the battle had wasted no time in starting and had gathered momentum rapidly. It seemed to be in full swing already. Guns answered each other from seemingly different distances, and Kangyr seemed to feel pain with every report.

"Are you sure you can?" Chet asked him quietly. "It is said that the Ketaxil have new weapons and plans of attack. Are you sure the ways you held them off before will work again?"

Kangyr started to say something but broke the first word off to listen to a particularly violent and rapid volley of gunfire. "I think so," he said finally, but there was a lack of conviction in his voice. "With the Supreme Presence on our side—"

"It might not hurt to have some of our magic on your side, too," Chet suggested. The distant rumble of battle continued to underline the conversation. "Take this boat, for instance. With the spirit-sticks mounted in bow and stern, it can fly high over the enemy. If nothing else, it could carry a messenger to a neighboring island for help when all the routes are blocked. The mere surprise of seeing such a craft could place the enemy off guard. No doubt Your Holiness could even find ways to use them in actual battle. Would you like to go for a ride and see how it works?"

"No," Kangyr replied at once, shrinking slightly away from the floater. "No, thank you. Perhaps later. I can see what it does. But . . . " He stared distantly at an icon of himself, much as Chet had seen him do once before. "From all sides," Kangyr said sullenly, "I'm besieged not only by Ketaxil but by people telling me I must adopt this or that newfangled contraption to protect my town. First Terek, now you—"

"Might I ask," Chet ventured cautiously, "just what Terek tried to get Your Holiness to adopt?"

"Guns," Kangyr said with a shruglike gesture. "New kinds of guns firing more rapidly, and firing larger balls to larger distances. . . . It would be impossible to aim such devices, of course, yet Terek claimed he could aim them better then our old guns—by doing mumbo jumbo with figures on paper!"

Hardly surprising, Chet thought as one of the old guns

coughed somewhere beyond the wall, *that he'd spend some time on trajectory problems—probably complete with fudge factors for air resistance and such.* He asked Kangyr, "Did you ever try Terek's methods?"

"Of course not! A dixar is no fool. And the ideas underlying Terek's wild scheme were so terribly at odds with the Truth. . . ." He broke off, and a flurry of cannon filled the pause. With an abrupt change of expression, Kangyr dropped the subject of Terek and looked with renewed interest at the airfloater's figurehead. "These spirits of yours," he said in a tone much like that he used when he first suggested that he would welcome magical help. "They are of the Supreme Presence?"

Chet wasn't sure how to answer that and was relieved to hear Tina, who had a somewhat better understanding of the Temple's beliefs and practices, fill in for him. "Of course," she said brightly. "Isn't everything?"

For the moment Kangyr seemed almost satisfied. Then he sank back into his mood of doubt. "Actually," he said slowly, "I hardly see the need of either. I know Terek's a crackpot and I don't see that your flying boat is any panacea. If it's true that the Ketaxil have better weapons, flying boats will hardly counteract them."

"Maybe not," said Chet, vaguely disappointed but deciding not to press the point until he had time to give it more thought. "But if you change your mind, we can get you many more such boats on short notice—"

He didn't finish the sentence because suddenly there was an insistent pounding on the door. Before Kangyr could react, it flew open and a Templeman ran in, panting from exertion. Chet recognized him as Xymrok, the one who had originally brought them before Kangyr.

"Your Holiness," Xymrok said excitedly. "Our guns are failing to repel them. The periphery is feeling unprecedented destruction, and—" Then he noticed the floater and broke off in midsentence, staring wide-eyed. "Your Holiness, what *is* that?"

Xymrok's report had had its effect. Kangyr's decision had been made with obvious reluctance, but it had been made. "Salvation," he said curtly, and then added under his breath, "I hope."

15

Terek moved swiftly through the streets toward the northern periphery, driven by the pounding of gunfire in his ears and the pounding of frustration and rage though his whole being. Most of the battle noise was still straight ahead, and off to his right, but there was no question in his mind of deviating from his course except briefly, to bypass specific dangers. There was no question about where he must go. . . .

He had been on the second terrace, near the southwest corner, when it started. He had seen Ravi yesterday, briefly; he had been unusually taciturn, acting almost as if he found Terek's company embarrassing. But he had given Terek permission to devote his time to whatever work he himself deemed most worthwhile. Grimly, Terek had decided that the Temple was still going to need his projectile work, whether it admitted it now or later, and wall or no wall.

So this morning—after pausing on the way here to stare at the thing in the sky which had so frightened the others in the marketplace—he had gathered his notes and gone out in the morning sunshine to continue and refine those calculations. He had found a spot where the Day Star could reach him directly, protected from the wind but not the warmth, and was just getting into the work when the first shot reached him.

He froze in the middle of an equation. The sound came from the northeast, of course; he was in the wrong position to see its exact source from here. He didn't even take time to return his papers to his chamber; there wasn't time. He hated to take the risk, but he could hide them so they would be fairly safe here for a little while. After only a few seconds' indecision, he lifted a heavy flat rock in a nearby garden enough to shove the papers under, then dropped it and took off at a quick jog north along the eastern rail. He heard three or four more shots as he ran, and caught a couple of quick glimpses of Ketaxil ships between the columns. But they were already too far west for a really good look.

Until he reached the northeast corner. There he stopped, panting, and leaned against a column to survey the view to the north. There were seven of the ships—far more than he had ever seen before—and they were already closing in tightly on the northern periphery.

Not far east of Terek's shack.

More cannon shots rang out, but these sounded closer than the others—even more so than should be accounted for by Terek's change of position. He found them by eye, black dots that had just been wheeled into an opening near his shack. He had seen them stored near there in recent days. . . .

Then he heard other shots, in sound much more like the first one he had heard. And coincident with them he saw flame and smoke spurt from three of the Ketaxil ships. With a sudden sinking feeling, he realized what had happened.

They had fired the first shots. The Ketaxil now had cannons. Either they had developed their own, or they were experimenting with captured ones from towns.

Either way, with the mobility their guns gained by being mounted on the ships, the Ketaxil did have the advantage that the rumors had claimed. The town was a sitting duck. And there were more ships than ever before, and, as the shiny black of the ash-tree leaves so strongly reminded him, winter was coming on. . . .

They would be in earnest this time.

Without further ado, Terek headed for the nearest stairs down. He had to get home and find out what was happening there. Ironically, with all his superior knowledge of weaponry, he had no actual weapons at his disposal. What he would do in a head-on confrontation with Ketaxil was a problem for which he had no ready solution. But he would worry about that when the need arose.

Now he was nearing the edge of town, more than a little afraid of what he would find there. Moments earlier, he had met Xymrok, half running along a periphery street toward the monastery, looking harried and scared.

"Disciple Terek," Xymrok had said, pausing with a show of concern (for, having done his time on the wall, Terek was momentarily in more or less good graces, at least officially.) "I hope your family is all right. We've never been hit like this before. Not at all like this. I must get word to the dixar Kangyr right away!"

He had started to run on and Terek had thought suddenly of the thing in the sky and called out, "Wait a minute, Xymrok." Xymrok had turned, listening but impatient. "I saw those outlanders go by a little while ago. The magicians. They were heading for the castle; you wouldn't believe me if I told you how. See if you can find out what's going on, will you?"

"I'll see," Xymrok had said with a puzzled frown, and then he had been off like a shot.

The air was filling with dark, pungent-smelling smoke, and the sounds of battle were growing louder as Terek approached the water. There were those he expected, of course—the sporadic barks and coughs of Keldac and Ketaxil cannons and, nearer, hoofbeats and cries of terror and pain in nearby streets. But there were new sounds, too, sounds which Terek had never before heard and did not know how to interpret. But they also came from the neighboring streets—loud, sharp, cracking sounds like small explosions. Hurrying between the rows of tightly closed and shuttered shacks, Terek tried to picture what the new sounds might be. He felt sure that they were not a good sign.

He found out suddenly. He was hurrying so single-mindedly toward his home that he didn't realize until too late just how close the shouts ahead were. He was out into the well square, standing unprotected and in full view, before he realized there was no longer anything between him and the battle. He took the street in in a single shocking glance. The reality of the milling Ketaxil and the mounted Temple lancers and the still bodies around the well barely had time to register before survival instinct catapulted him back into the street from which he had come.

Flattened against the wall of somebody's shack, shaking a little as he thought of how close the call had been, he looked out into the square. His view from here wasn't good, but they didn't seem to have seen him.

He looked around quickly, wheels driven by the Kemrek equivalent of adrenaline spinning furiously in his head, deciding his next move. His first impulse was to backtrack and detour around the square, hoping to bypass this band and get on to his shack. But the sooner he knew what the banging sounds were, the better, and this same group might give him the opportunity to find out. He had glimpsed an unfamiliar long thing of metal and wood in the hands of one of the Ketaxil. . . .

Maybe he could combine the two aims. Cautiously but quickly, he sidled along the shacks until he came to the next belt-street. Then he darted along that one, pausing to check each radial before he crossed it.

The third radial had a shack with a scraggly hedge between him and the square. After a split second's indecision, he turned down it and slipped into the shrubbery, crouching amid the stiff twigs and looking out at the square.

Such squares, scattered through every Kengmor town, were favorite gathering places for townsfolk; everybody had to get water. Apparently these Ketaxil, a handful discharged by a single landing boat and sweeping inland, had stumbled upon this one, either by accident or design, and seen in it an opportunity for sport. Plunder was their main goal, but that could wait a few minutes. They knew there was no booty worth taking in the periphery, but there were victims who could provide amusement on the way. . . .

Terek could see three of them from here, and he tried to keep from dwelling on them. But he saw too much before he could tear his eyes away. Two of the bodies lay by the near side of the well, one a young man, face down, the other a young woman with her neck bent back sharply, staring frozenly upward but seeing nothing—quite possibly a pair who had just recently occupied one of these shacks. Both of their clothes were torn and stained; a crossbow bolt jutted from the man's back, but Terek couldn't see what had killed the girl. The third victim, from here, was just a bare leg draped over the low rock wall around the square well, so small it might have been a child's. But the rest was submerged, and the water was so deeply colored with blood that Terek could see nothing in it. And he didn't try.

This many, at least, the raiders had cut down at this well alone. There might well have been others who had managed to escape in the moment of surprise when the Temple lancers had ridden in, catching the Ketaxil in the middle of their games. Now three of them rode their doral in frantic circles among the half-dozen tall, bearded barbarians, urging their mounts to kick and trample while they poked and clubbed with their long lances. The Ketaxil viewed even this as a game; they could have easily fled, but instead they stood their ground, taking potshots at the Templemen while laughing and shouting unintelligibly among themselves.

One of them was standing off by himself, watching the rest of the fray from the sidelines as he fiddled with the new thing Terek had seen. It had a carved wooden grip, or something, and strapped to that a long metal pipe, flared at the end away from the wood. It seemed to be hollow; its user was poking something down into it. Then he pulled out the poking rod and thrust it through his belt. He lifted the tubular thing and put the wooden end against his shoulder. At the last instant, Terek realized with sudden shock what it must be—a small, portable cannon. He looked wildly about for something he might throw—

The blunderbuss went off with a bang astonishingly loud at such short range. Something smacked into a wall not far from Terek, leaving a round hole. One of the Templemen grunted and toppled, slowly at first, from his dora.

Another, who had been about to skewer a Ketaxil crossbowman, whirled in involuntary surprise at the sound, missing his aim. His lance's intended target took instant advantage of his distraction to get off a bolt at the third Templeman. It struck him in the throat and he fell forward, clinging to his dora's neck, with an odd gurgling scream. The remaining Templeman, already distracted once, turned again. One of the raiders lunged, grabbing the shaft of his lance and twisting it so violently that the Templeman lost his grip and went flying from his saddle.

He landed on his belly, his wind knocked from him. Two other Ketaxil rushed in and kicked him over onto his back. One of them bent down and ripped open the front of his chest armor. The one who had pulled him down had picked up his lance and was now running toward its former owner. With a high leap, he brought the points down hard where the Templeman's armor had been. He was partly in the way, but Terek saw the blood gush from the Templeman's chest and heard his stifled cry, and when the raider let go of the shaft it still stood, vertical and unmoving.

Terek could watch no more. He left the bushes and dashed at top speed through a maze of little streets, looping around the square and giving that particular group of Ketaxil a wide berth. Luckily he met no more, though the sounds were never far off. In minutes he turned onto his own street.

And saw flames raging several houses down. He broke into a run, his worst fears welling up. For an instant they almost subsided a little when he saw that the flaming shack was not his own. But only for an instant, for as he rush past the flames he was that his home was no more. Its flames were almost finished.

He slowed to a stop in front of its remains, feeling sick and dizzy. A few tongues of flame still flicked forth here and there, but mostly that was past. It had not taken long. The old shack had caved in early, and now it rested below knee-level, a chaotic assortment of ashes and coals half smothered under pieces of roofing. Shaking violently, Terek found a long stick and used it to lift aside some of the half-burned planks.

The two bodies huddled together on the remains of the sleeping platform were charred beyond recognition, but there was no question of who they had been.

A fury rose in Terek such as he had never known before—at the barbarians and at Kangyr and at the meddling outlanders who were leading Kangyr away from the help he had offered to put an end to this.

For him—and for Dajhek and Tolimra—it was too late. But nothing like this should ever happen again. For two minutes Terek stood, staring at what had just minutes ago been Dajhek and Tolimra and home, letting the wrath and determination build. Then he turned and ran all the way back to the monastery, dodging Ketaxil wherever he found them.

He found Xymrok pacing back and forth near the northwest entrance, alone. That was good. Terek hurried up to him, masking his boiling feelings, and slipped him a ceramic coin. "Any word?" he asked, glancing significantly up.

Xymrok pocketed the coin and looked around. "The dixar Kangyr has accepted aid from the foreign magicians," he whispered quickly. "They have a strange boat which flies, and say they will sell Kangyr a number of these—"

Terek didn't wait for all the details. He pounded the door until another Templeman opened it from inside, recognized him as one enjoying slight and variable favor with the dixar, and let him in.

Then he started at top speed up the long succession of corridors and stairs, going out of his way only long enough to retrieve the notes he had hidden on the second terrace and conceal them in his garments.

The guard at the door of the dixar's chamber blocked his way. Terek stood two paces in front of him, glaring. "The dixar does not wish to see you now," the guard said stiffly, holding his gaze aloof.

"Are the outlander magicians in there?" Terek demanded. Even here, he could hear the sounds of strife in the town—but muted and faint, as if they didn't really matter up here.

The guard stared straight ahead without answering.

Terek waited, breathing hard and thinking. He could tell that things had changed out there. The action had moved inland; there was less of the deep cannon fire and more of the small arms and faint shouts of hand-to-hand fighting.

When the guard still said nothing, Terek said, "Won't you even announce me?"

"No," said the guard.

"But I have news about the Ketaxil. They do have new weapons—"

"The dixar has heard."

Terek said no more, but he didn't move—until he had planned his approach. Then he moved like lightning, diving under the guard's outstretched lance arm, throwing the door open, and half falling into the dixar's chamber. "Your Holiness," he blurted out, catching himself on the end of the table. "I have to talk to you—"

The guard's hand locked on the back of his neck. "I'm terribly sorry about this, Your Holiness," the guard stammered behind him. "I don't know how it happened. But I'll see that he bothers you no more—"

"Let him be," the dixar said quietly. His voice was very level; he was sitting with both forearms stretched along the arms of his throne, his face impassive. "I'll hear what he has to say this time. But leave the door open." He thought a moment and added, "And go down the stairs to the junction to wait. I'll call if I need you."

"Yes, Your Holiness." The vise on Terek's neck relaxed, and footsteps receded behind him. Terek waited, concentrating hard on controlling himself, until they were gone.

Then he spoke, his voice low and ominous. "You wouldn't listen to me, Your Holiness. If we had started in time, we might have been able to prevent most of this. Do you know what's happening out there, Your Holiness?"

"I know," said Kangyr, nodding slightly. That was all he said, but from the way he said it, Terek knew how heavily it weighed upon him. And yet—

"I don't believe you do," Terek said slowly. "Not really. You can't. Not up here all the time, sitting in this little box without even a window so you don't have to look at the world outside—"

"It would be *too* overwhelming then," Kangyr said solemnly. "The burden is great enough even this way. You don't understand, Terek, but—"

"*I* don't understand?" Terek exploded. "Your Holiness, I've just come from the ashes of my house. My parents were burned to death this morning. I had to look at them; you didn't. And you say *I* don't understand!"

"I'm very sorry, Terek," Kangyr said very quietly. "I really am. But it could not be prevented. Perhaps others will be more fortunate in the future. We're getting better ways—"

"Your Holiness," Terek interrupted, even more exasperated than he dared show, "you're being taken in. The magician's boats aren't going to save Yngmor, or even Yldac." Kangyr's eyebrows rose slightly, but Terek ignored that and went on. "Not by themselves, anyway. At best, they provide a way to carry word from one town to another. But what good is that if the Ketaxil have destroyed the towns? Face it, Your Holiness—we can't survive without better defense. And no matter what else you use in addition, that means better coast guns. And I can tell you how to make them."

Kangyr stared at him for a long time, his face full of weariness and uncertainty Terek had never seen there until quite recently. "Terek," he said finally, "we've been through all this before. Do you want to spend all your time on the wall?"

"I'll risk it," Terek said tightly, "if the alternative is to watch you throw away a chance to salvage some of what we call civilization." He paused. Then, "Your Holiness, what make you believe that these so-called magicians are infallible while everything I say is wrong?"

"Do I?" Kangyr snapped. "I don't think so. Why are *you*

so suspicious of *them*? 'Magnificent and infinitely varied—'"

"'—are the ways of the Supreme Presence,' " Terek finished quickly. "Yes. I know. But how is it that with the Supreme Presence everything is possible but what *I* suggest?"

"You're verging on blasphemy," Kangyr warned. "And you miss the point. It's not that way at all. It's just that you try to impose artificial restrictions on—"

"Your Holiness misses *my* point," Terek interrupted. "Okay. Maybe the foreigners' magic is real—*but that doesn't prove my work is wrong!* You preach that the Supreme Presence can act in any way it chooses—and I say that includes the ways I describe. But there's even more than that. Maybe nature can act any way it likes—but there are certain ways it seems to prefer most of the time, and there's strength in learning those. You believe that yourself."

"How dare you tell me what I believe—"

"It's implicit in your actions. Your discomfort at the thought of the flying boats is obvious. Why do they make you uncomfortable? Because they clash with your built-in ideas of how things naturally act. And you're *very* sure that everything revolves around Ymrek?"

"Yes!"

"Okay, let's leave that to argue about later. But meanwhile, give my guns a try." His voice lowered. "As for your magicians—I don't know how their tricks work. It doesn't matter. But, as dixar, haven't you wondered about the possibility that you're being enticed into a trap?"

Kangyr looked at him sharply. "What do you mean?"

Terek paused, momentarily hesitant to attack a man with his own religion. Then he said it. "You never did find out where they come from, did you? Yet, as you once reminded me, the Temple recognizes sources of power opposed to the Harmony of the Supreme Presence. And these people have hands like no others we've ever seen. I'd think you'd wait to deal with them until you know. . . ."

Kangyr looked startled, then pensive. For several seconds he was silent. Then he said grimly, "On *that* point, I'll have to agree with you. The question bears further examination."

Outside, the guns continued, though more sporadically than before. And there were shots and shouts so close that it was clear that some Ketaxil had at last reached the monastery.

16

The last guns stopped sometime during the night, having largely given way to the quieter sounds of systematic looting some hours earlier. In the morning silence lay over Yldac like a shroud, but the sounds of the raid still echoed restlessly in the Barlin's memories.

They sat outside, alone, on low folding stools placed close together against the invisible lower hull of the boat. They didn't speak; they hadn't spoken more than two words since they got up, earlier than the others. The thought had simply seemed to be in both their minds that they should come out here and see if there was any sign of how things had come out. They wouldn't actually be able to see the town beyond the thicket, of course—not even the castle—but still it had seemed somehow an appropriate thing to do. So here they still sat, staring off in the general direction of the town and turning things over in their numbed minds.

The morning seemed curiously harmonious with their mood. Sometime during the night it had rained; the water still stood in big globules on the grass. Now it was very still. A soft mist hung in the air around them, merging into a uniformly gray sky. Above the thicket they saw the tops of plumes of smoke rising very straight above the town.

A part of Chet's mind gradually came to reflect that there was something somehow strange about being able to see the smoke as well as he could. It took him a while to figure out what it was.

He was seeing some of the smoke—and, now that he knew where to look, even part of the castle—*through* the treetops. The ash trees, overnight had turned from gleaming black trees to bare skeletons. Looking at a small one nearby, Chet noticed a scattering of fine powder—like ashes—on the ground beneath it. Apparently the leaves, in their black phase, became extremely delicate, holding their shape until wind or rain came along and then crumbling completely. . . .

No, wait. Looking more closely, he saw that the leaves were still on the trees—or rather, shadows of them were, in black lace. The vein network remained intact; only the intervening tissue fell out as dust. He had never seen anything like that before, and he had not even taken time to look closely at one of the turning leaves before they fell. There was so much to learn about a new planet, and so little time to do it.

He caught himself wondering at the strange paths his mind was wandering. Then he heard a slight sniffling sound from Tina. "Don't do that," he told her gently, brushing a tear off her cheek. "You'll blow your cover."

She smiled slightly. "Sorry. I forgot. But I was just thinking about some of the things we saw yesterday. What a waste. And it could have been prevented, if either our methods or Terek's had been in use."

"Preferably Terek's," Chet half grunted. He got out his pipe and started fiddling with the tobacco. "But it's not our fault they weren't, of course."

"No," Tina agreed. "Not this time. But next time? I don't know. Chet, do you think we did any good yesterday?"

Chet got his pipe going and puffed on it several times before answering, mulling that over. Finally he said, "I don't—"

The hatch made almost no noise opening, but they noticed the sounds of instruments and voices filtering out. They both turned to look up at the hatch swinging out and the cabin beyond. Jem Wadkinz leaned out and said, "Oh, there you are. Don't know what I would have done if you hadn't been. Are you two coming to join us for breakfast?"

"Well," Kel said as he finished up and shoved his tin aside, "now what? Are you going to be ready to move on tomorrow afternoon?"

"I seriously doubt it," said Chet, relighting the pipe had filled and barely lit before Jem had called them in to breakfast. "The only thing I can see that's happened that might change anything is that the town was hit very badly yesterday. But I don't see how that affects our date with Kangyr." Kangyr had contracted for two airfloaters, for starters, both to be delivered at midday tomorrow. Actually, Chet could think of plenty of things that might have gone wrong—it was even conceivable that the dixar himself could have died in the massacre. But anything like that should have shown up most powerfully on the PFSU. It was probably safe to assume that Kangyr would be meeting them to accept delivery as planned, shaken by yesterday's events but if anything more anxious than ever for the floaters' aid. "And then," said Chet, "we'll have to watch for the reactions."

"But you're not expecting any trouble," Kel said hopefully. "So once we know they have the floaters and are ready to use them, we should be able to move on."

"I don't know," Chet said firmly. "We're going to have to think it out pretty carefully. Actually, right now I'd say Kangyr's response so hasn't been very satisfactory."

Kel frowned. "Why not? He's accepted airfloaters, hasn't he?"

"Yes," Chet nodded. "Tentatively and distrustfully, but hopefully. And that wasn't really the object of the expedition."

"Then what was?" Kel demanded with obvious annoyance. "I thought—"

Chet thought wearily that this time he wouldn't bother trying to argue with him. But before he had decided how he would answer, Tina said to Kel, "You remember what I said about the intuitive ideas of natural law they must have? The object of the expedition was to confront Kangyr with magic that defied those as thoroughly as the stuff he's already seen defied Terek's laws."

"Because," said Chet, "as long as we seem believable to him but contrary to Terek's ideas, we're perfectly acceptable and a handy way to keep Terek down. But if we can make Kangyr himself think our magic makes so little sense it must be just trickery—"

"I don't really see how you can hope to do that," Kel interrupted. "I was thinking about what you said about the Temple's First Precept—"

"Oh, he'd never openly *admit* he regards us that way," Tina nodded. "But if he *does*, whether he says so or not, it'll influence what actually gets done. If he decides our magic just can't be taken too seriously—if he has to look at it as something apart from either the Temple's teachings or Terek's innovations, so screwy that it neither supports nor refutes either one—"

"Then," Chet finished, "he might have to take a fresh look at Terek's ideas. We'd hoped the floaters might affect him that way, but they didn't. Our problem—fixing our own damage—isn't really solved until Terek has the chance we took away from him. And at the moment I can't see that Kangyr is any closer to accepting Terek's ideas than he ever was. Maybe even farther."

"You mean," Kel gasped, "you think you actually made things even worse yesterday?"

"Possibly. But—"

"I knew I never should have let you do it," Kel muttered. "I shouldn't have listened to your—"

"Calm down," Chet told him. "We may still be able to fix it."

"How?" Kel snapped.

"Obviously," said Chet, "still more of the same. The basic idea was right; floaters just weren't enough to do the trick. The prescription's the same, but a stronger dose is indicated."

"I see," Jem grinned. "We take them some of the most outlandishly magical things I can concoct. And I know some dillies. Liquids where waves show up in color and change color when they reflect or diffract . . . negative gravitational masses . . . even things for which the concept of mass is meaningless."

"That's the idea," Chet nodded. "The more the merrier. They ain't seen nothin' yet!"

By then Kel's lower jaw was almost on the floor in dazed disbelief. But this time he made no real effort to stop them.

They spent most of the day preparing things. By nightfall the aft stowage was bulging with three full-sized floaters, and Jem had filled a sack with an assortment of quasimaterials which should astonish virtually anyone not up on the most recent research in them.

The sky cleared during the night, and by midmorning, when they were ready to open the cargo hatch, Yldac reposed in unseasonable warmth under a silky blue dome. The three floaters were roped together, with the piloted one in the lead and Kangyr's pair trailing side by side behind it. Jem, Tina, and Chet all sat in the lead floater as Jem eased out the port, drawing the ropes taut. Stiv and Kel each lifted one of the other floaters and guided it out the hatch—easily, for their control elements were locked in positions that would nearly neutralize their weight. They would be simply towed, not steered directly, and they would drift and bounce about—but they would do so so gently that there would be virtually no danger of damage.

As soon as they were out, the hatch shut behind them and Jem eased the train up, climbing quite steeply to avoid dragging the towed floaters over the trees, but keeping the lead floater nearly level for the comfort of its passengers. Once they had cleared the trees, he applied a fair amount of forward power so they moved ahead with the floaters in tow following smoothly, climbing much less than before. This time there was less reason to try to be inconspicuous, and more reason to fly low for a good aerial look at the town.

Even in the sparkling sunshine, the view below was a somber reminder of the day before yesterday. The damage was extensive and obvious, its impact intensified by an oppressive stillness that still lay over everything. The periphery, particularly to the north, had many piles of black ashes and half-standing, charred walls where shacks had been. Few people ran fearfully into the remaining houses, because few people were out. Wall Street itself stood nearly empty, its stalls and shops looking almost as if a hurricane had swept through them. Scraps of straw and cloth blew lazily around in the light breezes.

Even the monastery had not escaped, they saw as they started down toward the spot where they were to meet Kangyr. Loose trash lay strewn about the courtyard; Templemen and Disciples were just beginning to pick it up. Several carved doors had been blackened by fire; that to one of the corner chapels lay flat on the cobblestones, ripped completely off its hinges. What had happened to the accumulated works within, Chet hated even to think about.

Kangyr had appointed a spot on a lower terrace for delivery of the floaters. Chet picked it out as they approached and saw four figures waiting there. One of them, by the purple of his robe, was Kangyr. The others Chet couldn't yet make out. He was mildly surprised at their presence, but only mildly. In making the arrangements, nothing had been said about others being with Kangyr, but neither had anything been said to the contrary. The delivery of the floaters had enough potential importance to the Temple that the dixar might well make a ceremonial occasion of it, though Chet was not at all sure about that.

But as they drew close enough for a better look, his curiosity changed to a puzzled frown. Tina cast a slightly worried look back at him. Two of the additional figures were armored Templemen with functional lances.

And the third, easily recognizable even though they had previously seen him only in make-up on the wall, was Terek.

Why?

Despite apprehension, they landed as scheduled. All four of the figures waiting on the terrace watched attentively as Jem eased their floater onto the pavement several paces in front of them and the two in tow settled lightly behind it. As soon as they were down, the armed Templemen stepped briskly forward and flanked the floaters menacingly.

Then Kangyr strode out to meet them, his lips pressed together with what might have been grim determination. He looked even paler and more shriveled out in the daylight than he did up in his chamber. "For religious reasons," he said crisply, without preamble, "I cannot conclude business with you until I have more definite knowledge of your origins. You will please answer the simple question: Where is your home?"

Chet felt stunned—and trapped. Somewhere along the line a new factor had entered the picture—and he wasn't sure what it was. There had been no hint of anything like this in their previous talks with Kangyr. None at all. He would have liked very much to take Tina aside and ask her for her ideas of what was going on. But of course there was no way to do that. It was up to him to answer. And his mind just kept darting back and forth in random directions, seeking but not finding anything it wanted to say.

"Quit stalling!" a voice rasped.

Chet looked up, surprised. It was Terek who had spoken, and there was an odd expression on his face. "Answer the question," he prodded. "You do have a home, don't you?" After a short pause, he turned to Kangyr. "He refuses to answer, Your Holiness. Our suspicions—"

Terek has something to do with it. Chet tried hard to focus his mind on the idea. Terek had said something to the dixar; somehow, it seemed, he lay behind this whole confrontation.

How?

Chet struggled frantically to pin it down. *If I were Terek,* he thought, *what would I want and what would I do about it?* The problem swirled, amorphous, spinning too fast to see.

Kangyr nodded gravely. Chet saw him give an almost imperceptible signal to the Templemen, and their free hands moved to their lances—

And the swirl clicked into place and stopped, and Chet thought he saw. He might be wrong, but there was no time to deliberate. "I'll answer," he said.

Kangyr's eyebrows shot up, he glanced at the lancers,

and they seemed to relax. Terek's expression changed abruptly to a rather bewildered one. He and Kangyr stared attentively at Chet.

Chet's pulse raced. He knew that Bydron Kel would never forgive what he was about to do, but he suddenly thought he understood what was going on.

And that, at this stage, however drastic it might seem, the rest of the answer might be as simple as the truth.

"I'll tell you where we came from," he said evenly. "The place is called Larneg. It is a planet which revolves about a very distant star—much as Ymrek revolves around the Day Star."

He heard Tina and Jem gasp, shocked. Kangyr's face registered first confusion, then disbelief, then anger. Terek's reactions were the most complicated—first, very briefly, he was stunned and incredulous, but then he believed, and with belief came a flood of satisfaction and excitement and humility.

"You're lying!" Kangyr snarled.

"I'm not," Chet said simply. "Terek knows. And we know that Terek is right, because we've seen both your world and ours from outside. Can you think of a more believable way to account for us and the things we do?"

Terek said quietly, "Coming here must have been very difficult—"

"Not for us," Chet said, "but it took our ancestors many centuries to learn how—even after our Terek's work was accepted." He addressed Kangyr. "There's a lot of what you could call magic in it. We have a lot more 'magic' that you haven't seen, and some of it could help you. But the kinds that can help you most, right now, are the same ones Terek can show you. *Let him*."

Kangyr stared at Chet, hard to read, for a long time. During that pause, Chet moved his hand inconspicuously to his beamer. Finally Kangyr said, "You will not leave. You will stay here and show us all this magic, and we will select what we want of it." He nodded to the lancers.

But before they could get their lances up, Chet had whipped his beamer out and they backed automatically away from it. “Stay put,” he said. “This little piece of magic can be deadly at a distance.” Nobody disputed him. They stayed put.

“We’re going,” Chet announced. “We’ll leave these two boats here, but they’re the last you’ll get from us. Whatever else you want, you’ll have to get for yourselves. Terek can get you started—and when we go, he’s your only chance. Make the most of him. There aren’t many like him.” Still holding the beamer rock-steady with one hand, Chet reached back with the other and disconnected the two new floaters from the one they were riding, “Let’s go, Jem.”

Jem lifted their floater off the terrace and started it almost imperceptibly skyward. “And if I don’t?” Kangyr asked sullenly.

Jem paused, holding the floater steady and turning his head so he could see both Chet and Kangyr. Chet grinned at the dixar. “I don’t think you’re that stupid, Kangyr. When you honestly ask yourself if you can afford not to try Terek’s suggestions, you won’t answer wrong. And one thing will lead to another. . . .”

He waited. When Kangyr said nothing, he nodded to Jem.

This time they lifted off in earnest and rose skyward with appreciable speed. Chet looked back at the dwindling figures on the monastery terrace and tried to foresee the future. There could be no absolute certainties in such things, of course, but—

It seemed as good a time as any to call their mission accomplished.

And now, with a people’s future hopefully salvaged, he would have to face Kel.

17

Kel was the very personification of smugness and righteous indignation as he sat primly at the end of Tomas Flangan's big ebony desk. He squirmed frequently in the deep, soft chair, and he kept dabbing with his cigarette at the silver ashtray on the corner of the desk. But through it all it was quite clear that he was now back in his element and confident that his word would finally—and justly—prevail.

Chet and Tina settled into the two similar chairs facing the Secretary of Extraterrestrial Life from across the desk. The dull shock of readjustment to civilization had not yet quite passed; bureaucrats and high stiff collars still seemed like elaborate and unnecessary nuisances. But they would have to deal with it. Chet settled back to wait, fairly sure he had a good general idea of what was in store. But neither he nor Tina said anything.

Flangan was frowning intently into the same packet of papers he had on their last encounter. But the particular documents he was looking at were new. Finally he looked up, the shiny spot on his bald pate shifting slightly as he did so. "I assume you realize," he said quietly, "that the charges Field Agent Kel has filed against you are rather serious."

"I'd expect them to be," Chet said evenly, "But before I say anything else, I'd like to hear exactly what it is we're being accused of."

"Reasonable," Flangan nodded. "Agent Kel?"

Kel drew himself up and crushed out his cigarette. "Willful misconduct and insubordination dealing with an alien culture on its home planet," he said clearly, looking straight at Chet. "Taking significant action in the field without approval of the field agent in charge—in particular, your decision to inform residents of Ymrek of our origins. An action which I hardly need to remind you is flagrantly illegal in itself and therefore constitutes a second count against you."

"I see," said Chet.

"You've heard the charges," said Flangan. "Do you deny them?" He looked at Chet, then at Tina, then back at Chet.

"I don't deny that I told them where we were from," Chet told him. "But I'd like to point out that I did it entirely on my own initiative. If those are your only charges, there's no way you can implicate anyone else." He saw Tina thinking, *But I would have been glad to do it myself.* But, of course, she knew better than to say it aloud unless it became clear that there would be some advantage in doing so.

"Hmph," said Flangan. "We'll debate that when the time comes. Meanwhile . . . you don't deny the charges. Do your realize their significance?"

"I think so."

"I hope so. Agent Kel is, in effect, recommending that you be declared unfit for field work. If I decide to so declare, you will be legally barred from future expeditions. I suppose you understand what that would mean. Not only the end of you career as you now know it, but possibly some rather unfortunate ramifications in your personal life. For instance, suppose I were to find that I agree with Agent Kel about your guilt—and that I also accept your claim of sole responsibility. Then *you* would be barred from field work, but your wife wouldn't. And if she chose to continue . . . well, you wouldn't even be allowed on the same planets where she worked."

Chet and Tina stared silent, unison daggers at him. Affecting indifference, Flangan took a plug of chew for himself, then held open the silver box out to Kel. "Bydron?"

"No, thank you, sir." Flangan drew the box back and put it away. Kel lit another cigarette.

"Now, then," said Flangan, leaning back and chewing calmly. "do you have some defense for your actions?"

"Of course I do," said Chet. "It was necessary."

Flangan raised his eyebrows slightly, very deliberately. "Oh? Please explain."

"Gladly. I gather you've already been through some version of the story. The problem remaining at the time we delivered the two floaters to Kangyr—stop me if you don't recognize anything—had two main aspects. The Temple didn't want to believe Terek, and it did want to believe us. Naturally we would rather have had it the other way. In accordance with the bureau's basic policy, we wanted to give such help as we gave with as little direct interference as possible. If we could encourage them to let Terek solve the problem we had planned to—"

"Come on, Barlin!" Kel broke in. "Quit trying to weasel out with double talk. I have you dead to rights this time. Over and over, out there, you kept working me into shady situations where I didn't like what you wanted to do but it wasn't outright illegal and I couldn't find enough alternatives to justify stopping you. I hated those times, and I hated you for getting me into them. But this time there are no two ways about it. You did what you did, you did it without consulting me, and it was flatly forbidden. What more is there to say?"

Chet stared at him. "Do you seriously mean to sit there and tell me that you intend to try to make a case out of the fact that I didn't ask your permission first?"

"Definitely."

"You weren't even there," said Tina. "How could he—"

"It was his duty," said Kel, "to arrange a delay long enough to talk it over with me." He stared sternly straight ahead.

Chet counted silently, forcing himself to ignore the blatant irrationality of the answer. If Kel was going to remain a field agent, he badly needed some real field experience—something like being forced to make an important decision under the immediate pressure of two Temple lancers and a conscience. But there was nothing Chet could do about that now. He looked coolly at Kel and said, "Okay, Agent Kel, let's argue it your way. Suppose I had asked you. What would you have said?"

"If you had asked, I would have taken time to give it the consideration it deserved and—"

"Why would you waste the time?" Chet interrupted. "You said yourself that telling aliens at that level of development where we came from is flatly illegal. Would you consider approving an illegal action?"

"I—" Kel began, obviously flustered.

Without waiting, Chet turned to Flangan. "Isn't it true, Mr. Secretary, that that particular action can *never* be authorized by a field agent? That approval must be obtained, if at all, from this office? And must be requested in person?"

Flangan nodded cautiously, "Yes," he said slowly. "That is the prescribed course—"

"So," Kel said quickly, "I would have said no. And if you wanted to pursue the matter, we would have had to come back here."

"And defeated the very purpose you were supposedly there to protect!" Chet pounced. "Rather ridiculous, isn't it, gentlemen? Think about it. Suppose I had managed to ask you. Suppose I had somehow managed to slip away without answering Kangyr—and to do it I might well have had to use my beamer, which neither of us would like. So we leave them, with or without two floaters, suspicious of both us and Terek and not really committed to either. We come back here and they have a few weeks for things to develop in our absence. Everything is so unstable that we can't predict how they'll develop, but the problem we created originally might well get even worse. And coming back to it after a few weeks, we'd not only find a situation that was radically different from the one we'd left, we wouldn't even know *how* it was different. Because we hadn't been watching while it developed."

He turned to Flangan. "You see what I'm driving at, Mr. Secretary? We're going to have to modify the laws. The present system simply isn't workable. I can see your reasons for insisting on a personal application for permission to intervene." (*Maybe even more of them than you want me to*, he thought parenthetically.) "But once you've committed yourself to doing it, the decisions have to be made on the spot as the emergencies develop. If you must have a field agent, he *must* have enough power to authorize whatever actions are needed. Even that one, and even retroactively, if need be." He looked pointedly at Kel and added, "But if he has that power, he also needs to be competent to use it."

Kel bristled. "Are you calling me incompetent, Barlin? You have no right—"

"Yes, I am," said Chet, "and I do have the right, because you are. Mr. Secretary, I trust you're transcribing this interview and that you'll go over it and take a close look at how much competence Agent Kel's parts of it show. He doesn't even know the laws he's supposed to enforce! And you'll find plenty of evidence in our trip records that he was bumbling along neither understanding nor really caring about the natives. The more we thought about it, the more astonished Tina and I became that a man like Kel could be given a position like that. Decisions that are going to affect the whole future history of a world have no business being made by petty bureaucrats. We'd like to see some reforms, and soon. So, yes, Agent Kel, go ahead and press charges of incompetence against me if you like. Just bear in mind that if you do, I'm going to return the favor. And you know what kind of a case I have." He paused briefly and then added, "And I'm not going to do it quietly. The whole Republic will hear what Tina and I have to say about the way this bureau's being run. If we have to, we're willing to gamble our careers on it. And yours." He turned back to Flangan and added quietly, "And even yours, Mr. Secretary."

Flangan stared at him with frank incredulity, but for a long time he didn't say anything. Chet looked back at Kel. "It's your move," he said softly. "The reforms we're going to work for anyway. If you want to make it a public comparison of incompetences, that's up to you. But if you want to reconsider . . . maybe we can work at it on a less personal plane. And more civilized." He waited.

Kel was staring at Flangan as if pleading for rescue, his lower lip trembling visibly. But the Secretary didn't even look at him. Finally Kel said weakly. "I guess there might be some advantage in that. If you're going to insist on . . . "

His voice trailed off.

Flangan nodded slightly, his eyes narrowed with distaste. "An ugly choice," he said. "But a type that must be made occasionally. Congratulations, Dr. Barlin. You have a stalemate. I'd be very interested in knowing whether your rash move did produce a desirable end result out there. I'll grant that it looks as if it may; I'll also grant that it's strictly illegal under the present law. Okay. Maybe we will have to change the law, and if that's the case it might be better to let this lie for a while. Personally, I'd still like to see the question of your competence answered, now that it's been raised, whether Agent Kel pursues his charges or not." He stared wistfully at his chew box. "Unfortunately, I don't know any way to answer it without a follow-up study—because the real issue seems to be whether your action really was justified by its results. And at the moment I'd hesitate to send *any* of you three back there, after the way you handled this one." He kept staring at the carved silver box, as if reflecting glumly on how little peace he was going to have in the last years of his career. Then he looked up, a haunted look in his eyes, and told the Barlins, "That will be all."

Chet and Tina stepped out of the building onto a moving strip that started them off toward their hotel. There was something subtly comforting in the multifaceted familiarity of the world—the quality of Capella's light, the patterns of the towers all around, the blended aromas of the Terran plants tastefully arranged along the strips. . . .

And soon they would be leaving the Capital and returning for the first time in months for an extended stay in even more congenial surroundings. There would even be relatives and old friends of their own species, which would be a very pleasant change of pace.

But Ymrek lingered in both their minds. They didn't talk much right after they left BEL offices, but when they had gone about a mile, Tina said quietly, "Chet, do you think things really will turn out all right?"

"With Yngmor?" said Chet, in the process of loading his

pipe. He pondered. "I think they'll make it. Not quite the same way they might have without us, but they'll make it." He thought silently for a few more seconds, puffing on his pipe and watching the blurred colors of flower patches streak by, then added in a stunned half whisper, "Or maybe . . . "

"What?"

"Or maybe things will turn out a *lot* different. Not necessarily worse, by any means, but a lot different. Something just hit me in a way it never did before, and I wonder . . . "

His voice trailed off again as they started across the deceleration strips near the hotel. As they stepped off the last one onto solid ground, Tina prompted him. "Yes?"

He stopped and looked at her. "This trip really drove home to me just how big a 'little' thing can be in its effects. Mainly in terms of making me a lot more leery of so-called little interferences. But all the way home I kept asking myself, 'Where would *we* be now if the apple had never fallen on Newton . . . or if it had been a quasi-apple?'"

She waited again. "And . . . ?"

"Well, now," Chet drawled as he started walking again, toward the hotel door, "I was just thinking. *Their* Newton knows about *both*."

AFTERWORD

Stanley Schmidt

Like most stories, *Newton and the Quasi-Apple* has convoluted roots. Also like most stories in my experience, it grew from not one major idea, but two—even though I initially made the mistake of thinking that one of them was enough to generate a story all by itself.

In February 1969, when I was a graduate student in physics and had just recently started selling science fiction to Analog, then-editor John W. Campbell published an editorial called "Sensational Discovery" that strongly tickled my imagination. It described some research he had recently seen demonstrated at Bell Labs that showed new ways in which human sensation is far more complicated than people commonly assume. In particular, he described computer-generated sounds that went up or down a scale continuously for as long as you cared to listen, and descending scales in which the last note, when compared directly to the first, was higher, even though straightforward logic said it had to be lower. John included in the editorial a picture of one of those visual paradoxes (see the corner ornaments on the "magic carpet" on the cover of this book!) that can be drawn but not built, and whimsically suggested that such a thing might be the sort of tuning fork that could produce sounds like these.

I was immediately struck by a startling analogy. The Bell Labs experiment showed that it was possible to artificially make sound waves with properties that could not be produced by any naturally occurring mechanical system. What if the same were true of other kinds of waves, too—including the ones that we normally perceive as matter? Thus were born "quasimaterials," a hypothetical class of artificial matter-like wave constructions with properties ordinary matter couldn't have: the ability to damp out and fade away; inequivalent gravitational and inertial masses; perhaps even to actually make a tangible, three-dimensional version of that visual paradox!

Now at this time I was, as I said, a graduate student in physics—and looking for an assistant professorship in a suddenly depressed job market. Given that, it's hardly surprising that my first story about quasimaterials was a satirical farce pitting the crazy properties of quasimaterials against the hardly less crazy foibles of academic politics. I had fun with it, but John Campbell said the idea was "too good to waste on such a trivial story line." I wasn't sure what else to do with it until the following fall, when I had that assistant professorship and for the first time found myself developing my own course and lectures.

There's a good deal of truth in the old saw that the best way to learn something is to teach it. As a physics student, I'd never fully appreciated the magnitude of Isaac Newton's accomplishment in formulating his laws of motion and gravitation. From my twentieth-century perspective, it all seemed so simple. But the night I was preparing my own first lecture about it, it suddenly hit me—hard!—what an awesome achievement it was for somebody who knew only what Newton knew in the 17th century.

It haunted my subconscious that whole night, and the next morning, when I was giving the lecture, something else happened. Right in the middle of it, something leaped out of my subconscious and demanded, "Could he still have done it if somebody had shown him quasimaterials that didn't follow his laws?"

I realized right away that that was the extra ingredient I needed to write a quasimaterial story I could sell John Campbell. I struggled hard to hold onto it so it wouldn't slip away before I finished the lecture, and then wrote it down before I even went back to my office.

The note in my pocket notebook was still a long way from

being a story, of course. I still had to create a Newton-analog to have this problem, and a culture for him to have it in, and another culture to throw the quasi-monkey-wrench in the works. Fortunately I had a head start on the last part, at least, in the form of a sketchy future history in which I'd already set some other stories, a couple of which I'd even sold. I had a lot of fun creating Ymrek and its peoples and then watching and recording what they did, and eventually I had a story called "Newton and the Quasi-Apple" which John was willing to buy.

He also gave it what I consider some of the most striking of Kelly Freas's many striking illustrations (which, regrettably, were not available for this edition of the book for contractual reasons, but I'm grateful to Roger MacBride Allen for getting some fine new ones from Taylor Blanchard).

John did one other thing that I wasn't quite as happy with, at least right away: He changed the title to "Lost Newton" without asking or even telling me. The first I heard of it was when I read the announcement of its publication in the preceding issue, and it took me a while even to figure out what the new title meant. But eventually I was glad for the change, because when I later fleshed the story out to novel length, I could get my own title back for the form more people would remember: *Newton and the Quasi-Apple,* with a different title for the short version to keep people from confusing the two. (Hm-m-m . . . could John have been anticipating that possibility and intentionally doing me a favor?)

Certainly the novel owes its existence to a couple of other huge favors. At a time when I'd only published a handful of stories and only met a couple of other professional writers or editors, I unexpectedly got the chance to spend a sizable part of a weekend with Gordon R. Dickson, a writer I'd long admired from afar, when I was vacationing in Florida and he was visiting fellow writer Joseph Green to research his novel *The Far Call.* I looked forward to the chance to meet him, when Joe (an astoundingly generous fellow) suggested I come by that same weekend, but I hoped Gordy wouldn't consider my presence too much of a nuisance. I didn't even expect him to recognize my name, so you can imagine my surprise when he not only knew who I was, but during evening bull sessions after his day's work was done started talking in great detail about what he liked a lot and not so much in my few published stories.

It quickly became apparent that Gordy, too, was an astoundingly generous fellow, and it was he who suggested flat out, "Why don't you expand 'Lost Newton' to a novel? There's a lot more story there than you've told." I said it was an intriguing suggestion, but I doubted that anybody would yet be interested in a novel from me and I didn't want to spend that much time and energy writing a big project with that little chance of selling. He patiently explained that I wouldn't write the whole novel on speculation; I should write the first few chapters and an outline of the rest, and get a publisher to give me a contract to finish the book. He even offered to look over my proposal to see if he had any suggestions about how to improve its chances. I took him up on that; and when a long time went by with no response, I feared he'd found it so terrible he was having trouble thinking of a diplomatic way to break the news to me. Then one night the phone rang and it was Gordy, telling me it was fine and I should go for it, and going on to chat for an hour (on his own dime, from Minnesota to Ohio!) about all manner of writerly things.

So I wrote the proposal, sent it off to the Scott Meredith agency in New York, and went back to working on other things. One day some months later one of my physics students tricked me into trying a cut-rate introductory flying lesson, knowing I'd be instantly hooked. As I drove home from the airport, having scheduled my next lesson and committed myself to an expensive course of instruction, I wondered, "Now how am I going to pay for this?" That very afternoon, my agent called from New York to say he'd sold *Newton* to Doubleday. Now all I had to do was write it.

That turned out to be more fun than I'd anticipated. It wasn't just a matter of padding, which I wouldn't have liked, but of getting to know my world and its people in more depth. And Kelly Freas had quite a bit to do with how it turned out. For one thing, he taught me a lesson with his cover. While writing the novelette, I had pictured Tina Barlin as a diminutive brunette, so when she showed up on the Analog cover as a statuesque blonde, I found the effect rather jarring. I was going to write Kelly and ask how he could have so ignored my description—until I realized to my considerable embarrassment that I hadn't provided one. Moral for writers: if anything about a character's appearance is important to you, you should mention it explicitly and early in the story.

Anyway, Kelly's painting was far more substantial than my original mental image, so Tina quickly became a blonde and remains one to this day, even in my mind (and yes, I still like her that way). More to the point, I described her that way in the book. Kelly also invented some details for his interior illustrations that I hadn't thought of, but liked so much that I wrote those into the novel, too. When I saw Kelly at a convention a little later and told him what I'd done, he said, "You bastard!" But from the way he was chuckling, I was pretty sure he was pleased; and a few minutes later he gave me one of the nicest compliments I've ever had on a story: "It's such a pleasure to be assigned a story that's fun to illustrate!"

And a few years later I got another that will be hard to top: a letter from a reader who had named his firstborn son after Terek. I'm not sure how I can ever hope to live up to that, but I at least hope you'll enjoy the story.

Stanley Schmidt
New York, July 2001
(With slight updates, October 2013)

About the Author

photo by Joyce Schmidt

Stanley Schmidt was born in Cincinnati and graduated from the University of Cincinnati in 1966. He began selling stories while a graduate student at Case Western Reserve University, where he completed his Ph.D. in physics in 1969. He continued freelancing while an assistant professor at Heidelberg College in Ohio, teaching physics, astronomy, science fiction, and other oddities. (He was introduced to his wife, Joyce, by a serpent while teaching field biology in a place vaguely resembling that well-known garden.) He has contributed numerous stories and articles to original anthologies and magazines including *Analog*, *Asimov's*, *Fantasy & Science Fiction*, *Rigel*, *The Twilight Zone*, *Alfred Hitchcock's Mystery Magazine*, *American Journal of Physics*, *Camping Journal*, *Writer's Digest*, and *The Writer.* He has edited or coedited about a dozen anthologies.

Since 1978, as editor of *Analog Science Fiction and Fact*, he was nominated 34 times for the Hugo award for Best Professional Editor, and won in 2013 for Best Editor, Short Form. He is or has been a member of the Board of Advisers for the National Space Society and the Science Fiction Museum and Hall of Fame, and has been an invited speaker at national meetings of those organizations, the American Institute of Aeronautics and Astronautics, and the American Association of Physics Teachers, as well as numerous museums and universities. In his writing and editing he draws on a varied background including extensive experience as a musician, photographer, traveler, naturalist, outdoorsman, pilot, and linguist. Most of these influences have left traces in his five novels and short fiction. His nonfiction includes the book *Aliens and Alien Societies: A Writer's Guide to Creating Extraterrestrial Life-Forms*, and *The Coming Convergence: The Surprising Ways Diverse Technologies Interact to Shape Our World and Change the Future*, and hundreds of *Analog* editorials, some of them collected in *Which Way to the Future?* He was Guest of Honor at BucConeer, the 1998 World Science Fiction Convention in Baltimore, and has been a Nebula and Hugo award nominee for his fiction.

In September 2012, he retired from editing *Analog* (after a longer run than any previous editor, including John W. Campbell), and now anticipates doing more of his own writing, as well as many of the other things mentioned above.

Also by Stanley Schmidt
from FoxAcre Press

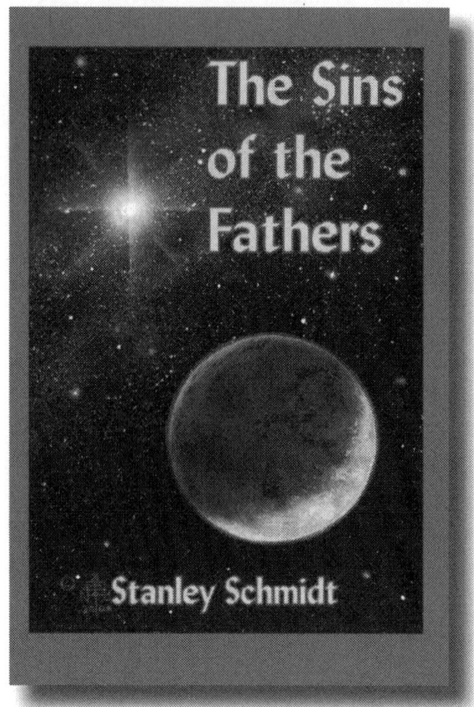

The Sins of the Fathers

Volume One of Stanley Schmidt's Classic Tale of the Planet in Peril!

A scientific expedition travels into deep space, and brings back shocking news: the galactic core has exploded—and the Earth is doomed! Includes a new introduction by Ben Bova, editor of the original *Analog* serials, plus the essay 'How to Move the Earth' by the author.

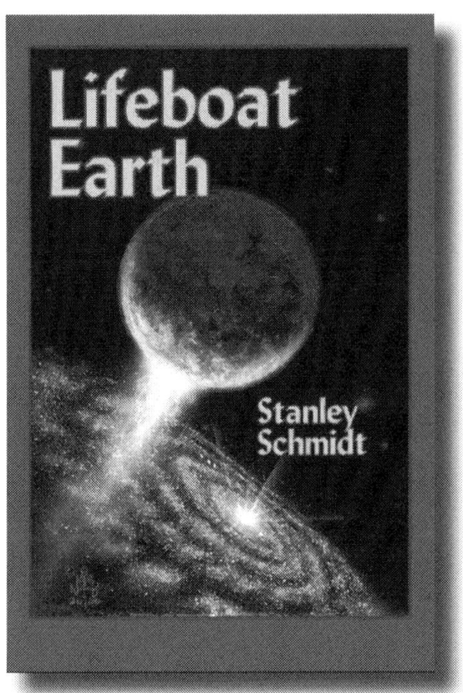

Lifeboat Earth

Volume Two of Stanley Schmidt's Classic Saga of the Planet in Peril.

The planet has escaped the doomed Milky Way—but who will survive a journey that could be as deadly as the radiation blast that will wipe out all life in the Galaxy? Includes a new afterword by the author.

Generation Gap
and Other Stories

Fascinating Short-Form Fiction by One of the Leading Editors in the Field

This brilliant single-author collection of stories comes to you from Dr. Stanley Schmidt, the long-time editor of *ANALOG Science Fiction / Science Fact Magazine*. Here are many of his favorite and best stories, ranging from the hardest of hard science fiction to the exploration of complex philosophical ideas. The author's introduction to the collection tells the stories behind the stories, explores his approach to fiction, and reveals one or two tricks of the trade along the way. It's a single-author collection that belongs on the shelf of every serious reader of short-form science fiction.

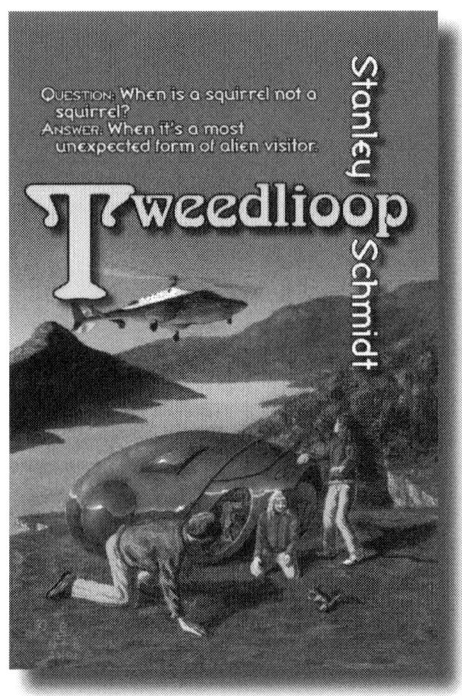

Tweedlioop

Will First Contact Be What It Takes to Make Us Know Ourselves?

Question: When is a squirrel not a squirrel?

Answer: When it's a most unexpected form of alien visitor. Stanley Schmidt's tale of First Contact will make you smile —and make you think.

FoxAcre
Press

www.FoxAcre.com

Manufactured by Amazon.ca
Bolton, ON

30322016R00118